Puffin Books

DIFFERENT DIRECTIONS

Most people would find it hard to cope with sitting in the same maths class as their mother, and Katharine feels furious to be put in such an impossible situation. She has her own problems – untameable hair, unattainable men, the usual sort of thing – without having to worry about her mother's maths homework. And then, to top it all, she hears people gossiping about her mother and the maths teacher, and even begins to suspect there may be something in it. Certainly Mrs Douglas has been very secretive lately.

But when Katharine finds out the real reason for the secrecy, it draws mother and daughter closer together and Katharine realizes she can be friends with her mother, and still lead a life of her own. She might even get some useful advice!

Theresa Breslin was born and now lives in Kirkentilloch where she is a branch librarian. She is married and has four children.

DIFFERENT DIRECTIONS

Theresa Breslin

PUFFIN BOOKS
in association with Blackie and Son Ltd

To 'O' Graders everywhere
– especially 4.0.

PUFFIN BOOKS

Published by the Penguin Group
Penguin Books Ltd, 27 Wrights Lane, London W8 5TZ, England
Viking Penguin, a division of Penguin Books USA Inc.
375 Hudson Street, New York, New York 10014, USA
Penguin Books Australia Ltd, Ringwood, Victoria, Australia
Penguin Books Canada Ltd, 2801 John Street, Markham, Ontario, Canada L3R 1B4
Penguin Books (NZ) Ltd, 182–190 Wairau Road, Auckland 10, New Zealand

Penguin Books Ltd, Registered Offices: Harmondsworth, Middlesex, England

First published by Blackie and Son Ltd 1989
Published in Puffin Books 1991
1 3 5 7 9 10 8 6 4 2

Text copyright © Theresa Breslin, 1989
All rights reserved

Printed in England by Clays Ltd, St Ives plc

ONE

Katharine Douglas looked out of the bus window at the figure running desperately towards the stop. A big baggy striped shirt flapped over bright pink leggings. High-heeled shoes and a large satchel did nothing to help the runner's progress. Katharine slid further down in her seat and silently prayed that the driver would not see the woman who was now shouting and waving frantically. The bus pulled away from the stop and gathered speed. Katharine straightened up and relaxed. Her mother was going to be late for school again.

'Wasn't that your mum?' said a voice behind her.

Katharine turned round. Spy McAllister from next door. Goody two shoes, father's only son, mother's pride and joy, yuk! would just happen to be sitting behind her.

'Really?' Katharine made a great show of peering out of the window. 'I didn't notice. Why didn't you tell me? For heaven's sake.' She stood up. 'Perhaps I should tell the driver, no, too late, we are on the dual carriageway now.' She sat down again.

Malcolm McAllister's face went a bit pink.

'Why don't you walk down to the bus stop together, anyway?' he asked.

Katharine stared at him. The boy was a fool. Walk to the bus stop together? She would look a real clown walking along the road in the morning beside her mother, whose taste in clothes made people turn their heads and stare. Then she would have to sit beside her on the bus and listen to her chattering excitedly about the classes she would have that day. And, worse still, be seen by the whole school going in the main gate together. No thanks.

'What a wonderful idea, Malcolm, why didn't I think of that? Then we could have a real girls' chat about make-up and boys and clothes and everything.'

Malcolm's face was bright red now.

'Kath, you are ridiculous, you know that. Other people would be proud of their mothers if they were doing what your mum is doing. *You* act as though she had leprosy.'

Katharine turned her head and stared out of the bus window. It wasn't the first time someone had said something like that to her. Which just proved that they didn't understand the situation.

She hadn't minded at all when her mother had said she was going back to school to try to get enough qualifications for Art College. What Katharine had not realised at the time was that it would be *her* school and *her* class which her mum would end up in. And not just any class. It would have to be smarmy Mr Hogg's maths class, who thought he was God's gift to women. He would lean over her mother's desk explaining the solution to a problem.

'Now, Angela, if you go over your working there and read these pages, I think it will become clear. And if you are stuck, I'm sure Katharine will help you out tonight.'

6

He would pat her mother on the shoulder before he walked away. A little habit he had developed recently that her mother appeared not to mind. Katharine gritted her teeth. How dare he call her mother by her first name, how dare he assume that she was going to do maths homework for her mother? She had things of her own to see to without doing her mother's work. Anyway, her mother was never going to pass 'O' grade maths—not in a million years. She did not have a logical mind, she was too scatter-brained. Witness this morning: she could not even get herself together properly to catch the bus on time. Not only that, she no longer had time to make Katharine's packed lunch, which meant eating vomit-inducing school dinners. Katharine scowled at her reflection in the bus window.

The bus rattled along the road and then made a sharp left turn to go through the town. It was very busy at this time in the morning. Cars, buses and lorries jammed the narrow main street. Despite the early hour most of the drivers were in shirt sleeves. A heat haze hung over the buildings, giving promise of a warm summer's day. The shopkeepers were pulling out their striped awnings, and the local café was setting out tables and chairs on the pavement.

The buildings in the main street were a mixture of old and new. A Victorian Schoolhouse, now the Town Library, and a Tolbooth and Steeple which dated back to the Middle Ages. The Old Kirk stood back from the road keeping a quiet composure among its gravestones. Outside its front entrance there were still set in the wall the iron jougs or rings fastened by a chain to the wall. This had been used as a kind of public rebuke system in times gone past. Wrongdoers would have to stand beside the church entrance with the collar round their neck while the congregation was assembling on a Sunday. Great trailing branches of blossom hung along the graveyard walls. Reserved and dignified, it maintained its atmosphere of serenity, despite the busy town about it.

Further along the street were its flashy new neighbours of chrome and glass, Woolworths and Poundstretcher, and then the Health Food Store, and Katharine's favourite haunt, The Body Shop. The long-promised-never-to-appear town bypass would put an end to the morning chaos, and no doubt ease drivers' tempers, but Katharine liked coming through the town each day. It gave her a chance to think and there was always something interesting going on. From her seat she could see down into cars and into offices and shops. Little cameos of life presented themselves to her, a still life caught in the moment it took the bus to gain a yard or so of space as the traffic hiccuped along the town. She breathed on the windows and drew a face on the glass, then rubbed it out again quickly lest anyone notice it. She could see two of her friends, Louise and Jane, walking to school together. She knocked on the window and waved as the bus passed them.

At the end of the main street, where the road forked, the bus climbed the hill towards the school. Katharine sighed. Another Monday and maths first block. Never mind, she smirked. She knew one pupil who was going to be at least half an hour late.

At the school gate Katharine hopped off the bus smartly to avoid Spy Malcolm, and walked towards the gate. A car drew into the bus bay and the door opened.

'Hello, darling. I just missed the bus this morning

but look who was passing and very kindly gave me a lift.'

Katharine gaped.

'Couldn't let our star pupil miss a precious second of maths, could I?' Mr Hogg called across from the driver's seat. Katharine managed a weak smile. Mr Hogg drove off towards the school teachers' car park. Mrs Douglas fell into step beside her daughter.

'When I was at school my maths teacher was a real ogre,' she said. 'Mr Hogg is such a pleasant man. I can't get over the way teachers treat pupils nowadays,' her mother went on, 'talking to you as though you were an adult.'

'You—are—an—adult, Mum,' said Katharine deliberately.

'Oh, I don't mean me. I mean you and your friends. Everything is so relaxed and friendly.'

Katharine rolled her eyes.

'I think it was when they got rid of the hand irons,' she said. 'You know, the ones they manacled children on to the slate and pencil with. I recall a distinct improvement after they were abolished.'

There was a silence.

'You know, Katharine, sarcasm doesn't always suit you,' said her mother. 'Excuse me, I have to go to the office this morning to collect some forms.' She went off down the corridor.

Katharine walked slowly towards the Upper School Cloakroom. Had she upset her mother? Difficult to tell. Her mother was usually very patient and even-tempered, but lately she had seemed on edge. Mr Hogg must be having a peculiar effect on her. Katharine shrugged her shoulders, and then, noticing Jane and Louise, quickened her pace to catch them up.

TWO

Katharine caught up with her friends and together they managed to insinuate their way through the crowd to the cloakroom mirror.

'Good grief! What a sight!' This was from Louise, as she rummaged in her bag for her essential equipment. Katharine looked at her friend. Short blonde hair, big blue eyes, clear skin, heart shaped face. If you threw a bucket of slime over her (and Katharine had on occasion contemplated this) she would still be every man's dream. Jane, on the other hand, was a more comfortable pal to have. Her hair was brownish and inclined to be greasy, and her face, at the moment, was erupting, nose, forehead, chin, with no regard for her sanity.

'I can't look,' she moaned. 'I spent *two* hours with a face pack on last night. I've tried Boots' best—every scientific preparation known to modern man, sorry woman, and still they come.' She touched her face. 'I can feel them, lying under my skin, all lurking there, and shouting to their wee friends on the surface, "Make room for me! Move over, move over!"'

Katharine sighed as she took her turn at the mirror. Spots were not her problem, not yet anyway, she thought bitterly. She stared at her face—not bad, a shade too long to be a perfect oval; complexion—few freckles, not too many, they could be covered; eyes—amber, different, but then she had decided this year that she was mature enough to know that being different could mean attractive. Her eyes travelled upwards to what should have been her crowning glory and she sighed again. Thick, coarse red hair was defiantly escaping from the combs with which she had trapped it this morning before leaving home. Two hair combs, six clasps, and a ponytail ribbon, she muttered to herself as she pulled them out and started again.

'Want to use some of this?' asked Louise.

Katharine surveyed the collection of mousses, gels, lotions and hairspray arranged along the window sill.

'No, thanks.' She brushed her hair viciously. She was convinced it had a personality of its own. It was a battle of wills and she was going to win, without any artificial help, thanks very much.

'You are destroying our natural resources with that stuff,' she said, her mouth full of grips.

'Yeh, yeh,' said Louise, 'that's why it rains so much here in Scotland. It's those spaceships the Russians send up.' She turned to look sideways in the mirror and smoothed her school blouse down into the waist-band of her skirt. 'I believe in taking all the help I can get.'

Ha! thought Katharine. Well, there I do have the advantage—a padded bra I don't need. She clipped the last grip in place.

'Aerosols which contain chlorine, fluorine and carbon are serious environmental pollutants. They accumulate in the upper atmosphere and deplete the ozone layer which shields the surface of the Earth.'

'Come on, you two,' said Jane, 'the bell is about to

go. Did you do all that homework Hedgehog gave us? I couldn't finish it, it doesn't make sense.'

'That is where you are wrong, girl,' said Katharine as she picked up her bag. 'Sense is precisely what it does make. Mathematics is an exact science. There is no room for airy fairy ideas as in guffy poetry. There are laws, and rules and it all fits neatly together, so there. It's what governs the Universe. It's a reassuring thing, it won't let you down, something you can rely on. It's not open to free interpretation.'

'Did your mum finish her homework?'

'Eh . . . I think so.'

'She really needs to get that "O" grade if she is going to College, doesn't she?' Jane went on.

'Actually, she doesn't. She is very talented and would probably get in on her art portfolio alone, but she thinks maths will help her with graphic design. Some hope! I think she is trying to prove something to herself, but she doesn't have an analytical mind. She's a very dithery person, lacks organising ability. We never know what we are having for dinner from one day to the next. She can't seem to plan ahead. She's too busy chatting to people all the time. I don't know why Mr Hogg keeps her in his top section—I think he expects me to help her with her work.'

'Do you think that's the only reason?' said Louise with a little smile. 'He spends a lot of time at her desk, and it's not always maths that's being discussed. Mind you, she is a very popular person in the school. All the men teachers ogle her, and everybody likes her.'

'Yeh,' said Jane, 'I like her. She's nice, your mum.'

'There's the bell,' said Katharine.

THREE

The maths class was no fun this morning, Katharine decided. Everyone was in a strange mood. Hedgehog was really putting the pressure on. 'Only a few weeks to the exams. The last run in,' he called it. He had spent some time with Mrs Douglas at the other end of the classroom. Her mother obviously had not been able to complete the weekend homework. Mr Hogg had not said anything to Katharine but she had caught his eye. He had raised his eyebrows and shook his head. It wasn't her responsibility—her mother hadn't asked her. Not that she would anyway, thought Katharine. I suppose I could have checked to see if she was doing it properly. Mind you, it was her mother's own fault. She hadn't spent enough time on it over the weekend. Sunday afternoon, when lunch was finished, she usually cleared the dining table and settled down to study for a few hours. Katharine, playing records in her room, remembered hearing her wandering restlessly about the house, tidying, she supposed.

Mr Hogg began to write on the blackboard.

Katharine sharpened her pencil and made a little mountain with the shavings.

'Right, pay attention everybody.'

Mr Hogg rapped his desk loudly with a metre stick.

'Today we will revise the equation of a line.'

He ignored the moans from the back of the class.

'If you all just look at the board, you can see I have already drawn there a straight line through the origin. The equation of this line is y equals x. The gradient is forty-five degrees.'

Katharine played with her pencil shavings on her desk.

His voice droned on.

Katharine had heard all this before. Her attention wandered. She looked out of the classroom window. From her desk, she could see from the old building into the new Art Huts. Another reason Monday morning maths was interesting. An uninterrupted view of Sixth Year Studies Art presented itself to her. Brian Patterson's hunky face frowned in concentration as he stood in front of his easel, brush in hand. He used his free hand to push his dark hair back from his forehead. A high, intelligent forehead, thought Katharine, a strong good-looking face. Far removed from pimply adolescent Fourth Years. What was he painting? Mrs Wallace, the art teacher was blocking her view.

Now that was a class she would love to be in. Her mum went across there after the maths lesson. She was putting together a folio of compositions for the College. The art students often worked on through breaktime. Maybe later on she could pretend she had forgotten her lunch money, mused Katharine. She would go across, open the door, pause for effect.

'Mother, I seem to have . . . Oh, sorry, I didn't realise there was someone else here . . . Brian, it is Brian isn't it? What are you working on? Well this is rather good, don't you think so, Angela?' She smiled to herself. What *was* he working on?

Katharine leaned forward in her chair to get a better view.

'Miss Douglas. Do you feel so supremely confident of passing your exam that you no longer need to pay any attention in class?' Mr Hogg was bearing down on her. 'What is so interesting out there that you are taking so much notice of it?'

There was a snicker from Louise.

'Nothing, sir. Sorry, sir.' Katharine bent hurriedly over her jotter.

'Mmmm.' Mr Hogg followed the line of Katharine's gaze. 'The people over there have already got their maths.'

Katharine felt her face flush. Small tendrils of hair took sneaky advantage of her confusion to make their escape. The clasp at the top of her head deliberately loosened itself and fell on to her desk. She picked it up and stuffed it into her pocket.

'I want to give you back your Multiple Choice results from last week.' Mr Hogg walked to the front of the classroom and, picking up a pile of papers, began to give them out.

Katharine glanced at her mark. Thirty-eight out of forty. She frowned and studied the two answers which were wrong. This type of exam was so simple. A well-trained monkey could do it.

'This type of exam is so simple,' said Mr Hogg, 'a well-trained monkey could do it. In fact scientific experiments have shown that by merely selecting answers at random there is an optimum lower limit.' He sighed. 'Some of us, however, do not manage to achieve this.'

In front of her, Malcolm reached out his hand for his paper.

'Malcolm the Monkey,' said Katharine audibly under her breath. It was out before she could stop it. She saw the back of Malcolm's neck turning bright red. Mr Hogg gave her a withering look. She hadn't actually meant it. She put a defiant look on her face and stared out of the window.

The bell for the end of the lesson signalled her release.

PE next block. Katharine got changed quickly. The boys went out on a run and the girls took the PE Hall for five-a-side football. Katharine got rid of some of her aggression by battering herself and the ball around the gym hall. Eventually Miss Carson blew her whistle and sent her off.

'Go and have a shower, dear, before you do yourself or someone else a mischief.'

As the cool water streamed over her face and down her body Katharine leaned her head against the tiles. What was the matter with her? She felt that she wanted to scream with rage and weep with frustration at the same time. She hadn't felt so emotionally upset about anything since her father had died. That was nearly six years ago. She should be well over that now. Well, not exactly over it, as her mother had explained. You don't really get over anything like that. You learn to live with it, adapt your life, and cope. Well she had, and did, until recently. So, what was her problem? She had an analytical mind, her teachers said so. She should be able to work out what was happening to her. Her mother . . . They had been very close then. They had clung to each other, quite literally, after the accident. What had changed? Her mother had changed, was changing. Katharine towelled herself furiously. She didn't mind at all her mother's return to study, despite the inconvenience to herself. It was annoying, that was all. Well, she had a right to be annoyed. Her exams were coming up, and having more to do at home held her back from studying. She pulled her clothes on. She felt better. When she rationalised things, she always felt better. She took her comb and went to the changing-room mirror. Perhaps she should take Louise's advice and saturate her hair with gel. Wet, it lay flat on her head; starting to dry it crept slowly into frizzy little curls.

'An environmentalist like yourself, Kath, should have no trouble in coping with hair like that.' Phyllis Calgary leaned conversationally across the sink and surveyed Katharine closely.

'Really?'

'Yes,' Phyllis said firmly. 'You hold life and nature sacred. I would have thought it was obvious. Become a Buddhist monk and have it all shaved off.' She cackled hysterically and went out of the changing room.

'Pig,' muttered Katharine. 'Bitch,' she said louder. The door of the changing-room had jammed open. 'Cow,' she shouted after the retreating figure.

'KATHARINE DOUGLAS!' Miss Carson appeared in the changing room. 'I don't know what's the matter with you today but you had better go along to the dinner hall now. Perhaps some food in your stomach will put you in a better humour.'

FOUR

The school dinner smell was creeping around the school, sliding under doors and withering flowers in vases.

'That's probably why I feel so rough,' thought Katharine. 'I've got this revolting muck to look forward to in the middle of the day.' Automatically she began to slow down, slurring her feet along the corridor. Most of her friends now patronised the school's new snack bar situated at the other end of the dinner hall. However Mrs Douglas was not impressed with snack meals. She had watched a TV documentary which (according to her) had proved conclusively that children with low intelligence and who were violent ate snacks. Or was it vice versa? Katharine couldn't remember. All she knew was that while most people were eating pizza and/or chips, she was stuck with meat and two veg. She sniffed the air. And the veg today smelled like . . . yes . . . as she had told her mother, as if someone had farted . . . it had to be . . . it could only be . . . Brussels sprouts. She groaned. The trouble was, her mother never sampled the dinners. She brought sandwiches and worked through the break.

She felt a sharp jab in the back.

'Hi!' It was Jane. 'Red card today? Naughty girl were we? *and* using foul and abusive language in the changing room. Tsk. Tsk.' Jane imitated Miss Carson's voice. 'We must all try to be patient with Katharine today. It is probably,' here she lowered her voice to a stage whisper, 'that *time* of the month.'

The two girls began to shriek with laughter.

Katharine found a free table with her plate of nutritional goodness, while her friends fought their way through the queue at the snack bar, standing on first years mercilessly. They joined her at last. Louise bit into her hot dog.

'Mmmmm. Delicious.'

'Someone murdered an innocent animal to produce that?' said Katharine bitterly. She looked down at her own plate. 'And I'm supposed to recharge my dilithium crystals on this.' She looked up. Her mother was walking towards their table with a full dinner plate in her hand.

'You don't mind if I join you? Do you?' she asked and sat down.

There was a silence.

'Er, no,' said Louise and moved her chair slightly. She glanced behind Mrs Douglas's head, and moved faster and further, scraping the chair legs on the lino. 'Definitely not. There is plenty of room here.' She gave Brian Patterson a huge welcoming smile as he pulled a chair over into the vacant place.

'Don't mind if I join you?'

'No, not at all,' said four voices together.

'I'm really ready for this,' he said. He started to eat his pizza.

'So am I,' said Mrs Douglas brightly. She speared

a Brussels sprout and started to eat it. A strange expression appeared on her face.

Brian examined her plate.

'You don't believe that traditional dinners are better for you?' he asked. 'It's a fallacy. Nutritionalists are beginning to think that a plate of chips midday provides necessary energy.' He took a long drink from his milkshake.

'Really?' Katharine beamed. She pulled her chair closer to the table. Not only was the boy talented and good-looking, he was brainy as well.

Her mother had stopped eating. She pressed a second Brussels sprout with her fork against the side of the plate. A cloudy liquid oozed from it. She bent her head over her plate and sniffed.

'You know, Katharine, you are quite right. These Brussels sprouts smell exactly as though someone has fa—'

'F . . . F . . . . Funnily enough,' said Katharine choking on a potato (were there no ends to which this woman would not go to embarrass her?). 'Funnily enough, I think I read that somewhere, what you said, Brian, about the chips I mean. They are definitely nutritious, in the middle of the day that is.' She was gibbering now. 'And pizzas, pizzas are good for you. I mean, look at the Italians, they eat tons of them. And they are great artists—Michelangelo, and . . . and what's his name?'

'Leonardo da Vinci?' suggested Brian helpfully.

'The very one,' said Katharine. 'See? Proves it. Great stuff, pasta.' She looked at Brian's place. 'And milk,' she finished.

He was smiling at her. He had a slightly puzzled look, but he hadn't actually run off to telephone the

Happy Wagon to come and collect her. And she had managed to avert yet another of her mother's public gaffs.

'Right, the two of you have converted me,' said Mrs Douglas. 'I know where this is going.' She picked up her plate and marched over to the waste bin. 'Would you like me to bring you something, Katharine? A pizza, perhaps?'

Katharine was studying the stylish way Brian held his milk carton. She noticed his fingers were stained blue and magenta with paint. Earth colours. They were two of a kind.

'What? Eh? No thanks. I'm not hungry.'

Jane and Louise had finished eating and so had he. What would be more natural than for them all to walk along the corridor together? The girls rose to their feet.

'Here, Brian,' said Mrs Douglas. 'I brought you a coffee from the machine.'

She sat down.

'I may be delayed a little this afternoon,' she said to Katharine. 'I have something to see to after school, but I should be home around five.'

'See you later then,' said Katharine with a fixed smile. Typical, she thought. Her mother was not content with Mr Hogg's attention, she had to monopolise Brian as well. 'She does that all the time,' she muttered to her friends between clenched teeth as they walked away. She kept her smile in place in case Brian was still watching them.

'Does what?' asked Louise innocently.

'Oh never mind,' said Katharine. Her stomach was growling with hunger and she was in a thoroughly bad mood. English literature with a teacher nutty about poetry lay ahead for the afternoon.

She would try, Katharine decided. This afternoon she would really try to understand the artistic imagination. After all, if she was going to develop a relationship with Brian Patterson, and she fully intended to have a darn good try at it, then she had better make an attempt to get on the right wavelength. She would pay close attention this afternoon. When Miss Travers started to talk about poems giving substance to thoughts and feelings, Katherine would make a determined effort to think and feel. When they discussed how symbolic imagery and poetic thought described subtle and ambiguous feelings, her eyes would not glaze over. The significance of the pattern of the poem would not escape her. She would carefully analyse rhythm and metre. There was a mathematical sequence to metre. After all it was only logical, wasn't it? Katharine thought as she went towards the English classroom.

FIVE

The final school bell rang at last and Katharine closed her book with a sigh. Miss Travers' face was slightly flushed. She must get a high on this stuff, thought Katharine. Beats me. Give me a little calculus, some tricky tessellations any day of the week. She turned to Jane.

'Truthfully, tell me, do you appreciate this?' She indicated the book.

'You mean you don't?' Jane picked up the book and opened it at random. 'Listen, dear.' She placed imaginary spectacles on the end of her nose. 'A poem is the expression of the soul. It is the deeper meaning of self—a thing of beauty. Something you gaze at in wonderment: a butterfly, a rainbow, Brian Patterson scoffing pizza and chips in the dinner hall.'

Katharine snatched the book from her friend's hand.

'Very funny. Ha ha. Are you going to the end of term disco?'

'Don't know. Are you asking me?'

'Why? Has anyone else?'

'Dozens, dearie. They queue up outside the cloak-room every morning. Unfortunately they are all little wimps in third year, and I am not that desperate—yet.'

'Come on, let's get out of here, things have been bad enough today without doing overtime. I'm starving. I'll have to make a quick pit stop at the café to refuel on the way home. Also, darling Mamma said she would be late tonight. It will give her time to reach home and get the dinner on.'

Jane shook her head sadly as she gathered up her bag and blazer. She began to imitate their guidance teacher.

'Katharine, dear, your emotional maturity is lagging behind your brain development. For someone with such natural intelligence you have very little sense of responsibility.'

Katharine's face began to colour. Too many people had been saying similar things to her for that to be funny any more. Malcolm next door, naggy Aunty Betty, her mother's sister, Mr Hogg etc, etc. Besides, Jane was one of a large family, and Katharine knew that she helped a lot at home. Her mother did shifts in a local knitwear factory, and on alternate weeks Jane walked her little sister home and prepared dinner for the family.

Jane looked at her friend closely.

'Hmmm. I diagnose pre-exam trauma, with further complications of unrequited love. Treatment consists of chocolate cream doughnuts, that is to say, totally pollution-free chocolate cream doughnuts, of course. She fingered her forehead. 'Well, pollution-free for some of us. Come on, the Toad will be waiting at the school gate.' She linked her arm through Katharine's and pulled her out of the classroom.

Kirsty, alias the Toad, was indeed waiting patiently at the school gate. She ran up as soon as she saw them and began to tell Jane all that had happened at her primary school during the day. Jane took her little sister's bag and slung it across her own shoulder as they walked down towards the town.

'Slow down. Slow down,' she laughed as Kirsty gabbled on. 'I can't make out what you're saying. The janitor was cleaning the Head Teacher? No? The Head was cleaning the janitor? No? I've got it. I've got it. The Head Teacher was *kissing* the janitor.'

Katharine felt a small pang of jealousy as she watched the two of them talking and laughing together. That kind of family closeness was something she was never going to experience. Unless her mother married again. An event which her aunt Betty kept reminding Katharine was not entirely out of the question.

'Your mum is a very attractive woman. She would be a good catch for any man.'

Her aunt still had the idea that females were some kind of fish. Anyway, she knew that her mum was pretty. Only too well. The way Hedgehog gazed at her in class was disgusting. A small hand slipped itself into her own.

'Can we go to the café?'

'Only if you promise to eat every bit of your dinner later, Toady. OK? What's on your menu tonight, Jane?'

'Mince. If it's Monday it must be mince. And potatoes, naturally. Get it, *naturally*?' Jane took in Katharine's scowl. 'Sorry, sorry. The mince was humanely slaughtered, honestly, died of old age in fact. Oh, Katharine, please don't lecture me. It's too warm today!'

They went into the café. It was very quiet. Perhaps everyone was rushing home to study. They paid for their food at the counter. Carlo, known as Chippie because his dad owned the café, was at the till.

'Saw your mum just now,' he said. 'Coming out of the Surgery. Mr Hogg dropped her off there earlier. They're very pally, aren't they?'

'What are you going to be when you grow up?' asked Katharine rudely. 'Inspector Gadget?'

She took her change and sat down. She shrugged her blazer off.

'It's becoming really clammy.'

'It's traditional,' said Jane, between mouthfuls of doughnut. 'By exam time it will be scorching. It never fails. The Education Board are in league with the weather men. They do it deliberately to depress you even more.'

Katharine put her hand at the side of her mouth.

'How about him?' she whispered. 'For the disco, I mean.'

Jane studied Chippie seriously for a moment or two.

'I don't know if the Latin looks are for me,' she said. 'Although I hear they are madly passionate. I only *hear* this,' she added quickly. 'However, if I lower my sights to second year I may get talked about.'

'What are you two whispering?' asked Kirsty. 'Tell me.'

'Certainly not,' said Jane. 'I can't wait long tonight,' she said to Katharine.

Katharine stood up.

'Neither can I. If you don't use this bus pass before 4.30 they charge full fare, and as I have just spent my money on junk food, I may have to walk.'

The three of them strolled along to Jane's house.

'It must be handy living here,' said Katharine, 'just off the main street.'

26

'Yes,' said Jane. 'I worked it out. I could rise at quarter to nine and be washed, dressed, fed and still be on time for school. Unfortunately that would only be possible if I lived there alone. The five other people in the house do tend to complicate matters.'

She said this cheerfully. She is a very happy person, thought Katharine. They reached the front gate. The garden was untidy, but in a friendly sort of way. A motorbike leaned against the side of the house and an old doll's pram was up-ended in one corner. At the end of the path was Toad's garden where she grew 'things'. Katharine peered over the hedge.

'What have you got growing today, pet?' She kept her face serious. Jane's little sister scorned traditional gardening methods. The results were too long to wait for, and besides which it was only boring flowers and plants which eventually appeared. Kirsty planted items from her toybox and other odd objects from around the house. She changed them frequently to add to the variety. Tonight there was planted firmly in the earth a tall screwdriver with a yellow handle: it was wearing a little mop cap. He-man and Shera stood side by side, along with an empty detergent bottle and a mug with a broken handle.

'Kath's proud of you, darling. Aren't you Kath? See—she's recycling the Earth's resources.'

'A few more people should do that, instead of chucking everything away when they're finished with it. If we all keep on doing that there will soon be nothing left to throw away.' She kissed the top of Kirsty's head. 'Us K's must stick together,' she said.

She walked back on to the main street and crossed the road to the bus stop. Her mother wasn't there. She must have caught an earlier bus, or perhaps

Hedgehog had given her a lift home. Chippie was right. They *were* becoming very pally. Katharine decided she didn't care. In fact she felt relieved. It was such a strain being in public with her mother. One never knew what she was going to say next. Like today in the dinner hall. Katharine shuddered.

There was a lamp on in the kitchen when she got home, but no smell of food cooking. Her mum was sitting at the table smoking. She jumped guiltily when Katharine came in.

'Oh, is that the time? I didn't realise.' She put the cigarette out hastily.

'What are you doing?' asked Katharine in amazement. 'I thought you gave that up ages ago. You only started anyway when Daddy . . . after the accident.'

'I know, sorry, I've got a lot on my mind.'

'Well, *that* doesn't help. It's polluting the atmosphere. Other people have to breathe it in. *And* it's a bad example to me.'

Her mother gave her a long look.

'Anything else?'

'Actually, yes,' said Katharine. 'You are behaving very oddly recently. I mean more oddly than usual,' she added. 'Things are slipping around here. It's a great strain on me. The exams are only a few weeks away.'

'I know the exams are only a few weeks away. You may remember I am sitting one of them, and trying to put together a folio.'

'Yes, yes,' said Katharine impatiently. 'Is that all it is? If you prepare work properly you need not worry about exams.'

'Not everyone has your intellect, Katharine. It

comes more easily to you than to the rest of us. It's a gift. Your dad had it. Anyway I have been studying.'

'Not recently. Yesterday you were mooning about the house.'

Her mother laughed.

'Is it only teenagers who are allowed to moon about?'

A light suddenly dawned on Katharine. Of course. She should have realised. They had had all this explained to them in Guidance Classes.

'Is it the menopause?' she asked. 'Is that what it is?'

Her mother laughed out loud in genuine amusement.

'Kath, really. I'm only thirty-seven years old, for goodness sake. I'm a young woman.' She glanced in the mirror above the dresser. 'Actually, I'm still quite attractive, I'll have you know. Mr Bates, the art assistant, told me so only today.' She patted her hair and batted her eyelashes. 'I was in the store cupboard and he came creeping up behind me in those soft rubber-soled shoes he wears. "Mrs Douglas," he breathed on the back of my neck, "you are a very attractive woman." He has a terrible sinus problem, you know, that's why he breathes so heavily.'

'Ha!' said Katharine. 'That's not the reason I heard why he breathes so heavily.'

'You may be right, dear,' said her mum. 'He has rather sweaty hands too.'

'How do you know that?' asked Katharine. 'You stay away from him in that store cupboard.'

'Don't worry, I have absolutely no intention of going near it again. I shall ask Brian to fetch anything I need. Now, *he* is rather nice, don't you think?'

'I didn't notice particularly,' said Katharine. 'Is there anything to eat?' she added quickly.

Her mother stood up. She opened her mouth as if to say something and then went over to the cooker.

'Do you think you could set the table?'

And Katharine, relieved at having been excused a heart-to-heart, did so.

SIX

Later on, when Katharine was slouched in front of the television she heard the phone ringing. She stood up, and with her eyes still on the TV screen, she slowly backed towards the living-room door, feeling for the handle behind her. By the time she had opened the door, her mother had answered the phone.

'Betty?' she said. 'Yes, well I saw him today. He said as soon as possible. I'll have to make arrangements for Katharine. Well, it's kind of you to offer . . .'

Katharine did not normally eavesdrop on other people's conversations, but her own name *had* been mentioned. She hesitated at the half-open door.

'No, I haven't said anything to her yet. I need to choose the right moment.'

Katharine closed the door softly and sat down on the couch. Her mind was whirling. She didn't want to hear any more. She hadn't liked what she had heard so far. 'I saw him today,' her mother had said. *Him*? Hedgehog, smarmy Hedgehog. It could only be him. Or maybe not. Maybe it was the art assistant. He was very interested in her mother's work, or her mother more likely. And the janitor, he was a widower, always talking about being on the look-out for a nice mother for his two children. Katharine shuddered. Well, she wasn't going to stay in the same house as those two repulsive brats, so they needn't think it. What had her mother said? 'Make arrangements for . . . for her . . .' with Aunty Betty, no way. Her cousin Meg was the most sanctimonious prat around. She remembered years ago, being on holiday with them at Saltcoats. Anything Katharine found interesting to do, like bringing crabs from the beach to swim in the bath of their small hotel, or changing all the labels on the suitcases in the hall, always had Meg running off clyping to Mummy about it. Katharine bit her nails furiously. If her mother was going to get married again then she, Katharine, would make her own arrangements. Jane, that was it, she would go and stay with Jane. There were so many of them in that house they would never notice one more.

'Katharine?' her mother was at the living-room door. Katharine jumped. She hadn't heard her come in. 'I'm going for a walk. Want to come? It's a lovely evening.'

'No,' said Katharine abruptly. She wasn't going to make it easy for her.

'OK. Er . . . That was Aunty Betty on the phone . . .'

'Really?' Katharine flicked the remote control between programmes. 'The odious Meg will be swotting for her Highers, I presume?'

Mrs Douglas sighed.

'Probably.' She paused. Katharine turned up the volume on the TV. Mrs Douglas looked at the TV and then at her daughter. 'I might call in next door for a coffee on the way back,' she went on, 'and have a little chat with Mary.'

Mrs McAllister, Malcolm's mother, would be getting ready to go to work. She did two nights each week at the Southern General Hospital.

'Mmmmm. Fine,' said Katharine.

Her mother sighed again and went out of the room.

Katharine heard the front door close. She turned off the television. The phone rang. She got up and walked into the hall and stared at it. It was probably *him*. She put her hand on the receiver and lifted it.

'Allo. Allo?' she said. 'Thees is the Free French Forces in Vichy France. Operator Yvette speaking.' Let him think there was insanity in the family—that might put him off.

'Oh, Kath,' said Jane. 'Thank goodness you're in. I need help.'

'Not as much as I do, pal,' said Katharine. 'You are not going to believe this. Can I come and stay with you?'

'That's what I really like about you, Katharine, darling,' said Jane, 'always ready to assist a friend with a problem.'

Katharine stopped. Was she so selfish? She swallowed hard.

'Sorry, sorry,' she said. 'What's the matter? Why did you phone?'

'This may seem incredible to you,' said Jane, 'but no one in this household, and that includes a student, one trained nursery nurse, a joiner, two parents and me, can do Toady's homework. What we have here is Devolution.'

'Devolution?' said Katharine. 'That'll be the day.'

'Devolution, dissention, something like that. Subtraction as we knew it. Primary four. You must remember. Take aways, greedy nine, and all that.'

'Yes, yes,' said Katharine. 'That is perfectly simple.'

'Well I have got news for you,' said Jane. 'They've

33

changed it. They are now operating a different system.'

'You can't change it,' said Katharine. 'That is the whole beauty of maths. It is constant. If you subtract one number from another, the answer is always the same. In primary four, anyway,' she added.

'Not now,' said Jane. 'This part of the Universe is off the wall. Hang on.' Katharine heard her speaking to Kirsty. 'It's called Decomposition. Have you heard of it? The way the Toad is carrying on it's as if she'll be boiled in oil if she doesn't get this right for tomorrow.'

'Decomposition? That's easy,' said Katharine. 'You have to think of the sum in tens and units, one column tens, the other units.' She struggled on, trying to explain the process which she found so simple. 'If the units which you are subtracting are more than the units which you have then you exchange a ten from the ten column to the unit column, where it becomes ten units. That is decomposition.'

'That's daft,' said Jane. 'You mean you are working left to right?'

'Well, sort of. Say the sum is 53 minus 19. That is 5 tens 3 units minus 1 ten 9 units. To take 9 away from 3 you must exchange a ten. Cross out the 5 and write 4, put 1 ten beside the 3 units. So instead of 5 tens and 3 units it becomes 4 tens and 13 units. 13 minus 9 is 4. 4 tens minus 1 ten is 3 tens. You arrive at the same answer as you would get doing it by the old system.'

She was rewarded with a squeal from Jane.

'She's got it,' Katharine muttered under her breath, 'she's got it. I do believe she's got it.'

'Right. I think I've got it,' said Jane. 'I'll go and try

to explain this to the family. By the way, what were you on about earlier?'

'Nothing,' said Katharine. 'It can keep.' She didn't feel that she wanted to discuss it now. 'I'll tell you tomorrow.'

She hung up. She went into the kitchen, made some cocoa and took it upstairs. She sat down at her desk and worked through some problems. The curtains were open and she could see clearly across the housetops. The sun was beginning to set below the rim of the distant hills. The air was cooling down as the heat left the earth. She and her mother had often in the past gone for walks at this time, along the river path to the town and back via the old railway line. A time to talk, or not. Comfortable in each other's company. The sky growing darker, wrapping its mantle about them. It was during times like this that Katharine had talked out her fears of going up to secondary school, her mother gently teasing her for being so serious. She had learned the facts of life on one of these walks. Katharine smiled to herself. All those strange adverts had suddenly made sense. She had felt so clever and important.

A plane flew over, making its slow descent towards Glasgow airport. The lights glowed in the night sky. It was almost dark. Katharine stretched to close her curtains. She saw her mother turn in at the McAllister's gate. She scowled. Another nattering session. The whole street probably knew about this forthcoming marriage except her. She undressed for bed. Her hair, released, sprang out round her head. She frowned at her reflection in her wardrobe mirror. Maybe Phyllis was correct. A crop, shaved all over. A few spikes at the top. She pulled a fringe down on to her forehead, tendrils of hair coiled round her fingers. She pulled her hand away impatiently, and threw her hairbrush on to the bedroom floor. She climbed into bed. She heard her mother outside their front gate talking to Malcolm's mum, who was getting into her car to drive to work.

'Don't worry, Angela. Katharine will cope. Try to think about yourself for a change.'

'HUH!' thought Katharine. Actually she liked Mrs McAllister. She had been a good neighbour and a friend after the car accident in which Mr Douglas had died. She had known Katharine's dad very well. He had been a bio-chemist doing research at the Hospital. Mrs McAllister worked some nights in the premature baby unit. Katharine had been there once that she could remember. Her dad had taken her when she was quite small. The babies all looked the same to her, little red beef links with tubes and wires attached. Mrs McAllister knew all their names and insisted they each had a definite personality despite being only a few days old. After Mr Douglas had died, Malcolm's mother had practically run their home for many months, shopping, cooking, cleaning. Katharine had played with Malcolm, who, unlike everyone else, refused to make any concessions to her. He won all the games they played and had even pushed her out of his treehouse, because he had said she was whining like a baby. She switched out her bedside lamp and lay smiling to herself in the dark.

When her mother came in later to say goodnight she was still smiling in her sleep, her hair spread on her pillow like a golden halo.

SEVEN

Katharine woke to the sound of someone moving about above her head. Her mother must be in the attic, which she used as a studio. It was very cramped but the light was good, with large windows which Katharine's dad had installed when they had first moved into the house. Until recently it had lain empty and spooky—like Miss Haversham's house, with long trailing cobwebs, and the dust everywhere. Her mother had been painting up there off and on for the last year, but never at this time in the morning. Katharine checked her watch on the bedside table— 6.30. She groaned. She would not get back to sleep now. The sun was bright behind the curtains and she could smell that early morning summer smell which promised a glorious day.

She staggered sleepily into the shower and stood under the spray for several minutes until she woke up properly. She washed her hair thoroughly and pinned it back while still wet.

'Right, get out of that!' she addressed it grimly in the bathroom mirror.

She went downstairs half-dressed. Nobody in the kitchen. Surely her mother had heard her get up. She must have heard the water running in the bathroom.

Grumpily Katharine began to make tea and toast. She heard the letterbox rattle as she banged cups and plates about.

'Postman,' she yelled upstairs as she collected the letters from the frontdoor mat. 'There's tea made,' she added grudgingly as her mother came into the kitchen. 'One for you.' She handed an official-looking brown envelope across the table.

Her mother read it hastily and crumpled it into the pocket of her smock.

'Anything important?' asked Katharine between mouthfuls of toast.

'Not as such,' said her mother evasively. She was very subdued this morning, thought Katharine. No wonder, if she had stayed up half the night painting.

'Were you up all night painting?' she asked. 'It's not good for you.' Nor for me, she was going to add, but thought better of it.

'Em, no,' said her mum. 'I just thought I'd get an early start today.'

'But you have all of today to paint,' said Katharine. 'You don't go to school on a Tuesday.'

'Yes I know, but I have a lot to do and I didn't sleep very well last night.'

The memory of last night's overheard telephone call came back to Katharine. Not surprising she couldn't sleep, thought Katharine. Probably too busy planning her honeymoon or something. She rose from the table.

'I'd better go,' she said.

'You have plenty of time,' said her mum. 'You could stay and talk for a while.'

Katharine hesitated. Perhaps she was being a little too hasty. After all her mother was entitled to her own life. It was the principle of the thing, though. She should have been consulted before this.

She glanced at the kitchen clock.

'I'll have to go now. I hate rushing for the bus.' This was true, she told herself. She preferred to pack her schoolbag carefully and saunter down to the bus-stop.

Her mother smiled brightly.

'OK, dear. I'll see you tonight, maybe we can have dinner in the garden.' She pulled up the kitchen blind. 'It's going to be a scorcher.'

Later, at lunchtime, Mrs Douglas's forecast proved correct. Louise, Jane and Katharine lay stretched out on the grassy slope overlooking the school playing fields, eating salad rolls which they had bought at the school snack bar.

Louise squinted at the sun from behind mirror shades.

'I see what you mean now about the ozone layer, Kath. I'll have to go inside. I'm beginning to burn.' She brushed the grass from her skirt. The three friends went inside the cool building.

'Aha, what's this?'

Jane was examining a notice on the main board.

'Tickets for the end of term disco will be on sale tomorrow!'

They sat down at the foot of the steps leading to the Assembly Hall.

'What do you think?' asked Jane. 'Shall we risk it? I know they don't deserve our presence, our style, our repartee, but one has to slum with the peasants occasionally?'

'Has anyone asked you yet?' Louise fanned herself with an exercise book.

'No,' said Katharine.

Louise looked relieved.

'Me neither,' she said. 'How about you, Jane?'

'Who is going to ask me with a face like this?' said Jane. She fingered her spots.

'You could always wear a paper bag over your head,' suggested Katharine.

'Be sure you make it a conservation-conscious, save-a-tree paperbag,' said Louise.

'Shall we make a pact,' said Jane, 'a solemn vow? We shall all go together, and then no one will be left out?'

Louise hesitated for a second.

'Yes,' she said.

'Yes,' said Katharine.

'Yes,' said Jane. 'Shall we sign in blood?'

'I don't think we need to go as far as that,' said Louise.

A small first year pupil ran up.

'Are you Louise Jordan?'

'And if I am?' Louise inspected him from over the top of her sunglasses. 'What does an insignificant little reptile such as yourself wish to know for?'

'You've to go to the Art Huts right away. Mrs Wallace wants to see you.' He ran off.

Louise sat up slowly. She adjusted her glasses.

'If this is Brian Patterson asking me to the disco,' she said, 'all deals are off. Understood?'

Jane turned to Katharine as Louise went away.

'What were you in such a flap about last night?' she asked. 'You wanted to come and stay in my house. Are you out of your mind? You would have to share with Kirsty and Stephanie. What's wrong, trouble at t'mill?'

Katharine lowered her voice.

'This is strictly confidential,' she said. 'I think my mother is going to get married.' She paused for Jane's reaction.

'That's terrific!' said Jane. 'I'm so pleased for her. She deserves to be happy again. Is it someone we know?'

Katharine was astonished. This was not the response she had expected from her best friend.

'I don't know who it is,' she said crossly. 'That's part of the problem. Don't you think she should have consulted me?'

'Consult you? Why?' Jane giggled. 'You mean ask your permission, dahling?' She spoke in a pompous voice, 'Katharine Douglas, may I have your leave to ask for your mother's hand in marriage? Oh, it's so romantic, Kath,' she sighed. 'Who could it be?' She stopped suddenly and gaped at Katharine. 'You don't think it could be Hedgehog, could it? Miss Carson in PE will be after your blood. She's been mooning over him for years, don't you know that, and she's not getting any younger, dearie. They used to say that he had "Carson's last chance" written in invisible ink on his back.'

Katharine was becoming increasingly annoyed as Jane wittered on. She was quite relieved when Louise appeared as the Lunch Bell rang.

'Are you all right, Louise?' she asked. 'Your face is bright red. What did Mrs Wallace want?'

'Listen to this,' said Louise. She paused for dramatic effect and positioned her sunglasses on top of her head. 'I have been chosen as the model for the sixth year studies Art Exam.' She collapsed on to the Assembly Hall steps. 'What am I going to wear? How am I going to do my make-up?' She covered her face with her hands.

'Didn't she tell you what you would have to put on?' asked Katharine, as they filed into Modern Studies.

'No, she said she would leave it up to me. It will be a surprise for them, she said. "But don't make it too big a surprise, Louise, dear," she also said.'

'We'll have a committee meeting,' said Jane. 'After Modern Studies,' she added quickly as she noticed Mr Jack glaring at them. The Modern Studies teacher was trying to pick teams and topics for the school's mid-week lunchtime debate.

'As you three seem to want to talk you can make up one team,' he said. 'And to be completely sexist we will have an all male team opposing.' He indicated Malcolm McAllister and a couple of his friends.

'Don't let the side down, lads,' he said.

'What is the topic, sir?' asked Malcolm.

'Yes, that might be helpful,' said Mr Jack. 'Katharine, you choose a subject dear to your heart.'

'Pollution,' said Katharine at once.

'Very good, very good. We will make it "Waste not, want not!" How about that? Really original, don't you think?'

The class groaned.

'Now, remember the agreement,' said Mr Jack. 'You all turn up tomorrow, even though it is lunchtime, and I let you away early last block on Friday. Meanwhile, heads together for a quick discussion and let's run over some debating techniques.'

By the time school was finished, Katharine's blouse was sticking to her back with perspiration.

'It's always the same,' she moaned, as they left the school gate and headed towards the town. 'You freeze in there in the winter and fry in the summer.'

'Anyone want to take a quick look round the shops before going home?' asked Louise. 'I want to get some ideas about what I could wear for modelling.'

'I can't really.' Jane indicated Kirsty.

'I'll come,' said Katharine. She caught sight of Jane's crestfallen face. 'Tell you what, why don't the two of you come up to my house later. We could try some stuff on you there, Louise. My mother has some way-out relics of the swinging sixties and all that. We have a legitimate reason for a get-together. We can say we are going over material for tomorrow's debate. I'm sure my mother won't mind.'

Jane's face brightened. 'That's a great idea. I will have some peace and quiet, and for one evening someone else can do Toady's homework.'

Louise was very excited. 'That would be fantastic, Kath. I'd be very grateful. Your mum would probably have some good suggestions.'

'Right,' said Katharine. 'I'm going to catch the early bus and I'll phone you later on.'

EIGHT

'You didn't actually wear these, Mum, did you?' Katharine had been rummaging in the back of the big wardrobe in her mother's bedroom and had brought out a pair of platform-soled shoes. She fastened on the ankle straps and hobbled to the full-length mirror. 'You must have looked like Minnie Mouse.'

Jane and Louise shrieked with laughter.

'Look at this,' said Louise, standing up. She had put on a pair of bell-bottom jeans and a flowery blouse.

'Peace, man,' said Jane.

'I'll have you know I was thought of as being trendy at one time,' said Mrs Douglas huffily.

'This could never have been trendy,' said Katharine picking up a large floppy hat, 'ever, at any time.'

'Just you wait,' said her mother. 'In a few years time this will be all the rage again.' She placed the hat on Louise's head. 'What do you think?'

'I don't want them to burst out laughing when I enter the room,' said Louise.

Mrs Douglas turned her round and studied her for a few minutes.

'Mmmm, you're right. That isn't really you.'

'What do you think is the real me?' asked Louise. 'Meryl Streep, Raquel Welch, Madonna?'

Mrs Douglas shuddered.

'No.' She thought for a bit. 'The real you is what you want to be ... combined with what you are, I suppose. Life is a compromise between what you want and what you can get. The trick is to appreciate that. Be all you can be without hurting others to achieve it.'

She framed Louise's face with her hands. 'To me you look like a Botticelli angel ... but the wings may prove difficult, and I have a feeling that you would prefer something a little more dramatic. No?'

Louise nodded.

'Right. How about this?' She opened one of the fashion books that were lying on the bed at a page showing the styles from the 1920s and 1930s. 'A flapper girl? A Bright Young Thing?'

'I don't know,' said Louise doubtfully.

'Put this on.' Mrs Douglas brought out a fringed sequined twist dress. 'We'll put little kiss curls all round your forehead. I'll do your make-up and then you can decide.' She pushed Louise away from the mirror. 'Don't look until I'm finished.'

With deft strokes, Katharine's mother applied base, shadow and rouge. She then carefully painted in a crimson cupid's bow on Louise's mouth. She stood back and surveyed her work. And then added a beauty spot just below the eye.

'There,' she said.

'Louise, that is fantastic,' said Jane. 'Honestly, brill, pure ex. Isn't it, Kath?'

Katharine gazed at her friend. She didn't realise her mother had such skill.

'It's great, Louise. It doesn't look like you at all.'

'Thanks very much, Kath,' said Louise. 'We can

always rely on you to say the right thing.' She went over to the mirror nervously and inspected herself.

'Goodness, I see what you mean.' She walked back and forwards and turned around. 'Do I have the nerve to wear it?' She pulled at the dress. 'It's a bit short, isn't it? And bright. Don't you think it's too loud?'

'Definitely not,' said Jane. 'It's just right. They won't know what's hit them.'

'It is good, Louise, honestly,' said Katharine. She thought of Brian Patterson, painting at his easel. 'I wish it was me.'

The wistful note in her voice convinced Louise.

'OK,' said Louise. 'I'll risk it.'

Mrs Douglas opened a carrier bag. 'Here, give me the dress. You take it home and let your mum see you in it. If you have any accessories such as long white gloves or a headband with a feather, experiment with them. When is the exam? Monday? Wear your outfit in the house a few times until you are comfortable in it. Now . . . I thought you three were going to work on the debating speeches for tomorrow? Come on downstairs to the dining-table and I'll make some hot chocolate and toast for you.'

In the dining-room, Katharine pored over the information she had collected from the library and the Body Shop.

'Do you know how much Britain would save per year in imports if we increased our use of recycled paper?'

'No,' said Jane. 'But I have this feeling that I am about to find out.'

'£400 million pounds,' said Katharine.

'Let me see that,' said Louise. 'That's colossal.' She began to read the leaflet. 'Here's an interesting item.

"Save rags for a local rag collection." Do you think if I gave all my clothes away and told my mother it was because I was trying to save the Earth she would buy me a new wardrobe?'

'Don't be so flippant,' said Katharine. She snatched the leaflet out of Louise's hand.

'Sorry,' said Louise. She took it back gently. 'I didn't think about it seriously before. It is quite ridiculous that we do throw so much away. It is . . . irresponsible, isn't it?'

'Yes,' said Mrs Douglas coming in the door with a tray. 'I remember when I was young, my mother used to open up the tea and sugar packets and shake out the last few ounces. Your Aunt Betty and I used to laugh. We thought it was because her family had been very poor. In fact it was only good sense. We hardly threw anything away. As children we made skilts from syrup tins.'

'What?' asked Katharine.

'I'll show you.' Mrs Douglas went out and returned from the kitchen with the tin of hot chocolate powder. 'We used two large tins such as this, say treacle or national dried milk tins. When they were empty, we would drill two holes in each one, at the top on opposite sides. Then you thread some strong string through, long enough to loop in your hand when standing on the tin. Beats skateboarding any day.'

'You didn't walk about on those, did you?' asked Jane.

'Walk? My dear girl, I ran. I was the street champion when I was ten. From the post-box on the corner to the lamppost at the other end.'

'The Leerie still lighting the street lamps in those days, was he?' Katharine enquired sweetly.

Mrs Douglas cuffed her daughter gently on the head.

'Here is something in one of the books Mr Jack gave us,' said Jane. 'Recycled glass is used in road building. Britain only recycles six per cent of its bottles, other countries recycle thirty per cent. We should have a bottle bank here.'

'You used to get money back on jam jars,' said Mrs Douglas. 'A ha'penny, I think it was.'

'For heaven's sake,' said Katharine. 'What is this? All our yesterdays?'

Jane held an imaginary microphone under Katharine's mother's nose.

'May I present the famous Lady Douglas, who has only just received her telegram from the Queen. Tell the viewers about your childhood m'lady and what you think is wrong with the world today. Modern Youth, perhaps?'

'No,' said Katharine's mother. 'I don't agree with that. Modern youth are much more environmentally conscious than I ever was. It's the adults today who have started to spoil the world. The future is in the hands of the children. I only hope they don't lose their idealism, and are able to channel their energy in the right directions.' She looked straight at Katharine.

'Hear, hear,' said Louise.

'However,' added Mrs Douglas, 'they might consider practising what they preach by losing the notion that it is somehow uncool to be seen returning a few empty lemonade bottles to the shops.' She picked up the tray and walked out of the room.

'Ouch,' said Jane.

'She's right,' said Katharine, 'you can't say things without following them through.'

The girls worked on for an hour and then Jane and Louise decided to go home before it became dark.

Katharine watched them from the gate walking down the road to the bus stop. Small clouds of midges swarmed under the chestnut tree in the garden, and the air was heavy with night-scented stock. She breathed in deeply and turned to go back into the house. Her mother was coming from the kitchen.

'Thanks for your help,' said Katharine awkwardly.

'Any time,' said Mrs Douglas. 'I'm going to bed early. Will you make sure everything is locked up?'

She hesitated and then gave Katharine a quick hug before going upstairs.

NINE

'The motion is,' Mr Jack announced next day at lunchtime, 'that this House thinks that "Once is enough".' He raised his eyebrows. 'I would like to add that it was Malcolm who decided on the wording of the proposal.'

The lecture theatre was almost full. Pupils were sitting on the stairs and squatting on the floor. Katharine, Jane and Louise felt very nervous on the platform. This was a completely different situation for them.

'Standing up in class and speaking out is going to be a dawdle after this,' whispered Jane.

Louise's face was going white and red in turns.

'There is nothing to it,' whispered Katharine. Her own stomach was churning, but she felt as team leader that it was her duty to try and inspire confidence. 'Just pick on one person in the audience and address yourself to them. That's what my mum told me this morning.'

'We should have rehearsed this,' moaned Louise. 'You should have told us to rehearse.'

'I did tell you,' hissed Katharine. 'You were supposed to go home and practise in front of the mirror last night.'

'Yes, well I feel that I have a slight advantage over you two in that respect,' said Jane. 'I made my whole family sit and listen to me. That is almost the same number as is here today.'

Katharine gave her friend a grateful look for trying to ease the tension.

'Anyway,' said Katharine, 'look at them.' She indicated the opposition. 'They don't look too confident to me.'

At the other side of the platform Malcolm and his two friends were having a quick consultation. The paper Malcolm was holding was trembling in his grasp and the three boys seemed to be arguing.

'Everything all right?' enquired Jane solicitously.

'Couldn't be better,' said Malcolm at once. 'You lot might just as well go home now.'

'I've found someone in the audience to focus on,' said Louise.

Jane nudged Katharine. Brian Patterson had come into the room at the back.

Mr Jack tapped the gavel on the lectern.

'Order, order,' he called. 'May I call upon the first speaker, Malcolm McAllister, to propose the motion.'

Malcolm got to his feet. Katharine noticed that he gripped the lectern tightly.

'*Blue Peter*,' he began loudly, 'has given Britain a great heritage. The youth of the United Kingdom, to a man, yes, ladies and gentlemen, I repeat, to a man, now know forty-five things they may do with an empty washing-up liquid bottle. Some of us,' he indicated the opposition, 'may even know forty-six.'

It was a good speech. Katharine had to admit that grudgingly. Witty and pertinent, Malcolm had argued a case for economic growth. By spending more, we created more work to keep others employed. He pointed the finger at the opposition who said one thing but did another. He claimed to have emptied the bins in the girls' cloakroom and senior girls' common room.

'"Waste not, want not," is their maxim,' he said. He held up a bag which contained empty tins of deodorant, hair spray, etc. He shook it in front of the audience. 'The next line of that saying is "Practice what you preach". Do they do this? Gentlemen and ladies, I say, no!'

The audience cheered.

'And now to conclude,' said Malcolm. 'I would like you all to think of the earliest case of recycling in history. The first known instance of using a component from a perfect invention to produce something else. May I present,' he swept out his arm to encompass Katharine, Louise and Jane, 'recycled rib! May I ask you to think where the troubles of the world have come from? May I remind you when you come to vote on the motion, that for the Creator himself, "Once was enough".'

Malcolm sat down. There were rousing cheers, and whistles and cat calls from the boys ranged along the window sills of the lecture room.

Katharine made a few notes and stood up. She faced a sea of people, mostly talking or still laughing at Malcolm's closing statement. She felt her nerve fail. Some teachers were standing at the back. Mr Jack smiled at her in encouragement. She noticed a movement at the back of the room. Her mother. Katharine swallowed. Her mum held her gaze for a second and then frowned and nodded to her. Katharine started to speak.

'Rubbish!' she said. 'Rubbish.' She paused. 'I am

not, of course, referring to my learned friend's speech. I am talking about the mountains of garbage which each of us, each year, throws away. Around ten times our own body weight, in fact. At present, less than two per cent of this is recycled. It could be much, much more. It is a national scandal that there is no government provision made for the collection of waste paper. One tonne of recycled newsprint saves one tonne of wood, that is about twelve trees. A newspaper like *The Sun* with a circulation of four million uses the equivalent of four thousand trees daily. Yes, four thousand. Now it is a matter of personal opinion whether you consider *The Sun* to be worth even one tree. The point is, over eighty per cent of household rubbish can be used again.'

Katharine went on to explain how other countries were leaving us behind in the environmental field. 'From next year all vehicles produced in West Germany will be fitted with anti-pollution devices. Britain has refused to join the "30" club, which includes all the main European countries as well as the Soviet Union, committing themselves to a thirty per cent cut in sulphur emission. Our waste is choking Europe,' she argued. 'We are killing forests, acidifying lakes, rivers and streams and soil. The lakes of Scotland have suffered more damage since the Industrial Revolution than in the preceding ten thousand years.

'If we allow these present trends to continue,' said Katharine, 'our landscape and wildlife will disappear. Governments say that we cannot afford to, I say that we cannot afford *not* to. We know what to do, but we lack the political will and personal commitment to do it. I want to read to you from the book *Ecology 2000* in which Tom Burke says ". . . We have to bring our ingenuity, our inventiveness to bear on the crisis in which we find ourselves. We face, as perhaps no other civilisation has faced, a choice of direction".'

The room was very quiet as Katharine sat down.

'That really broke them up,' whispered Jane.

The other speeches were shorter and provoked more comment from the audience.

'Well done, team,' said Katharine as Louise, the last to speak, sat down.

She noticed Brian Patterson was now standing beside her mother. He bent his head to say something to her and she smiled at him.

Mr Jack put the motion to the House. The boys present voted for the boys' team and the girls for Katharine, Jane and Louise. All except Brian Patterson. Katharine noticed that he had voted for them.

'Look,' hissed Jane, 'Brian Patterson voted for us.'

'Did he?' said Katharine.

'Right,' snarled Mr Jack. 'We will take the count again. We are not a bunch of bigotted sexists. You will vote on this motion properly. Now, again, please.'

The boys all voted for Malcolm and his friends, and the girls for Katharine's team.

Mr Jack started to foam at the mouth.

'I will not count the votes,' he declared. 'But before the bell rings I would like to compliment both teams. Malcolm for putting up a very good case for a difficult point of view, and Katharine for avoiding the trap of too much sentiment, and for giving us the hard facts. Credit too for the supporting speakers for their skill in picking up on points and on their ready wit. We will go into the inter-schools debating tournament this year with confidence.'

People had already begun to drift off, but the teams

on the platform were trapped until Mr Jack finished speaking. Jane rolled her eyes. Thankfully the bell rang. Katharine looked about for her mother but could not see her.

TEN

'Your speech was quite good, Malcolm,' said Katharine as the class were settling down for English next block.

'Yes, I thought so,' replied Malcolm airily. 'It combined humour and eloquence, with wit and sensitivity. I was rather pleased with it. Yours wasn't too bad, either,' he added.

Katharine laughed, and they chatted with an easy camaraderie which she realised had been missing from her life these last few weeks.

Mrs Travers commented on the debate.

'It was very good—excellent. You all did well,' she said. 'You do know, of course, that a good debating technique is to use quotes which I noticed that you did. Now I would like you to select quotes from *Macbeth* and learn a selection for use in your exam. Don't all choose the same ones. Read through a passage carefully and think of the relevance of each.'

She strolled about between the desks.

'Still flushed from your success, are you?' she asked Louise. 'Or are you excited for another reason. I hear you have been chosen as the model for the Sixth Year Art Exam.'

Someone gave a wolf-whistle from the back of the class.

'Have you decided what to wear?'

There was a snigger.

'If anyone is going to be childish,' said Mrs Travers, 'they can go next door and join Mr Jack's class and explain to him why they were sent.'

Katharine noticed that Louise's face was very red and that her hands were shaking.

'Mrs Travers, I don't think Louise is well.'

'I think you are correct, Katharine. Would you like to take Louise to the medical room, please?'

Louise stood up and swayed slightly.

'On second thoughts,' said Mrs Travers, 'I think I had better take her myself.'

She paused at the classroom door, one arm under Louise's shoulder supporting her.

'May I remind you that you are the Fourth Year and can be left unattended for a short while. I presume that you are past the silly stage where you all throw rulers and rubbers at the blackboard when the teacher leaves the room.'

She went out of the door and closed it behind her.

There was a pause, and then a hail of rulers and rubbers bounced off the blackboard.

Jane got up and flounced to the front of the classroom.

'I'm telling,' she said. She extended her arm straight out and wagged her finger dramatically, pointing to her classmates.

'I'm telling,' she chanted. 'I'm telling the teacher on Malcolm McAllister.'

She bent down to pick up her own ruler. The door opened and Mr Jack sent her sprawling.

'May one enquire what all this noise is and what you are doing down there, Jane?'

'Quotes,' said Jane scrambling to her feet. 'Quotes. Mrs Travers asked us to revise quotes from Macbeth.'

She held up her ruler.

'"Is this a dagger which I see before me, the handle toward my hand. Come let me clutch thee. I have thee not . . ."'

'Thank you, Jane,' said Mr Jack. 'Perhaps you would be good enough to pick up all these other daggers and return them to their owners.' He surveyed the room grimly. 'I will leave this door open. I want to hear the steady hum of brains working and nothing else. If I have to come back,' he paused, 'be warned— I take no prisoners.'

'I've found a good quote,' said Malcolm as Jane sat down. '"What are these so withered and so wild in their attire". I'll give you a hint. It applys to a group of people.'

'I wonder who they could be,' said Jane.

'Fourth Year boys out on their weekly jog?' suggested Katharine.

'Here is one for you, Kath,' said Phyllis. '"Don't shake your gory locks at me."'

Katharine felt her face flame red.

'"By the pricking of my thumbs, something wicked this way comes",' murmured Malcolm softly.

Katharine glanced across at him. He winked at her. She bent her head and tried to concentrate on her work.

Mrs Travers did not appear by the end of the session. Mr Jack set them some work to do as homework and dismissed them.

They sauntered along to the maths class. She would see her mother there, thought Katharine, and ask her what she thought of the debate. Malcolm was behind her in the corridor. She slowed her pace until he caught up.

'Hi,' she said.

'What bloody man is that?' he asked.

'Eh?'

'Don't you recognise a perfectly genuine Shakespearian quote when you hear one?' he asked.

'Shakespearian quotes were causing me a bit of embarrassment earlier,' said Katharine. 'And unfortunately with my type of colouring I can't hide it.'

'A beamer, I believe, is the term used by the First Years,' said Malcolm. 'I have the same problem. It's the red hair.'

'You don't have red hair,' said Katharine. She studied him. 'It's brownish, more sandy, really.'

'Red,' said Malcolm firmly. 'I've reconciled myself to it. He ran his fingers through his hair. I used to hate it, but we are quite good friends now.'

'The other day,' Katharine said slowly, 'in maths, the remark about the monkey. I didn't really mean it. It just slipped out.'

'I know,' said Malcolm kindly. 'It wasn't even me Hedgehog was talking about. I got quite a good mark. I just happened to put my hand out for my paper as he was speaking.'

'Why didn't Hedgehog say something?' said Katharine. 'Who was it that failed so badly?'

'You mean you don't know?'

A horrible realisation dawned on her.

'My mum?'

'Don't you talk to each other in your house?' asked Malcolm.

'Yes, no, sometimes. Oh, I don't know, Malcolm,'

said Katharine miserably. 'Things haven't been the same recently.'

To her shame Katharine felt her eyes filling with tears. She brushed her hand across her eyes.

Malcolm punched her on the arm.

'It will be OK. It's your wee hormones at work, upsetting you. Besides which,' he said slowly, 'I don't know if your mum is very well.'

'What?' said Katharine in alarm. 'Why do you say that?'

'It's only an impression I've picked up from my mum. They've been having big pow-wows in our kitchen lately.'

'Oh, that,' said Katharine. 'I thought that was to do with . . .' She stopped. She couldn't tell him what she suspected. Perhaps she had been mistaken in what she had heard on the phone. 'I'll have to make arrangements for her . . .' Had she jumped to the wrong conclusion in her usual quick-tempered way? She started to walk more quickly towards the maths classroom.

The lesson began. Her mother had not arrived. That was not unusual. She was frequently late for classes. Mr Hogg smiled at her when she arrived, breathless and apologetic. Though normally if a pupil came in late he was unsympathetic and sarcastic.

Katharine kept glancing at the door and her watch. Where was she? She was never as late as this.

'Katharine, dear,' said Mr Hogg, 'are you anxious about something? You keep checking your watch and the door. You won't have enough time to place a bet on the three-thirty today.'

The class tittered.

'Actually,' said Katharine hotly. 'I was concerned

about my mother. Even *she* is not usually as late as this.'

Mr Hogg gave her a puzzled look.

'I thought you knew that she was not coming to maths today. She told me she was meeting your Aunt Betty. The head said that she would be off for a few days. I am to give you some work for her to do at home.' He stopped. 'I assumed that you knew all this . . . perhaps you and she should have a little chat when you go home tonight.'

Fortunately for Katharine it was only ten minutes until the final bell. She did not think she could have sat still any longer. She flung her books in her bag and called to Jane.

'I'm going for the early bus home to have a little chat with Mummy,' she said between her teeth. 'There is something going on, and I am going to find out what it is.'

The bus took ages to get clear of the town. Ambling along the main road, the driver in shirt sleeves, whistled cheerfully, his window open, determined to enjoy the good weather. Katharine got off at the end of her road and hurried home. She could hear voices in the kitchen as she opened the front door. Her mother and Aunt Betty.

She crashed her school bag down on to the floor of the front hall.

The voices in the kitchen stopped and the door opened. Aunt Betty stood there.

'Hello, Kath,' she said. 'Long time, no see. Goodness, you've grown.'

Katharine pushed past her into the kitchen, where her mother sat at the table. She seemed white and tense.

'Hello, dear,' she said. 'You're home early today.'

'Yes,' said Katharine. 'And there is a reason for it.' She indicated Aunt Betty. 'Why is she here? Why were you not in the maths class this afternoon? Why are you going to be off school for the next few days. Why is it that Hedgehog and half the world know our business and I do not? *What* is going on?'

ELEVEN

Aunt Betty had followed Katharine into the kitchen. She addressed Katharine's mother.

'Angie,' she said, 'you *have* told Kath that I am staying for a few days?'

'Staying for a few days?' repeated Katharine. 'Where? Here?'

Aunt Betty looked at Mrs Douglas.

'You haven't told her, have you, Angie?' She shook her head. 'I thought you said you would.'

Mrs Douglas spread her hands out in a helpless gesture. 'I tried to, sort of.'

'This won't do, Angie.' Aunt Betty said severely. 'Both Mary McAllister and I offered to talk to Kath, and you said, no, you would manage.'

'This is too much,' said Katharine angrily. 'You're acting as though I wasn't here.' She sat down and looked directly into her mother's face. 'What exactly do you have to tell me. Are you afraid of me or something?'

'Not of you, dear, but of something, yes.'

Someone knocked on the back door and came in. It was Mrs McAllister.

'Saw the car, Betty, and heard voices, and I thought you might have arrived . . .' She stopped. 'Awkward moment?' She turned round. 'I'll come back later.'

'No, wait,' said Mrs Douglas. 'I got a letter yesterday and . . . eh . . .' She exchanged anxious glances with Aunt Betty.

'For heaven's sake,' shouted Katharine. 'What letter?'

Mrs McAllister jumped and gaped at Katharine.

Aunt Betty gave Mary McAllister a meaningful look.

'Angie hasn't spoken to Kath yet,' she said.

'Oh, Angie,' said Mary McAllister, 'you said you would.'

Katharine opened her mouth to scream.

Aunt Betty held up her hand.

'Stop!' she said. 'Mary and I are going next door for a cup of coffee. You,' she pointed at her sister, 'are going to talk to Kath. She is not a child any longer.' She went and stood beside Katharine and placed her hand on her shoulder. 'She is a young adult. Apart from which, she has a right to know. I am in full agreement with her. You should be discussing your problems with her before telling other people. She has every reason to be angry with you. Katharine has had to grow up quickly in these last years, and she obviously can shoulder responsibility. We will be next door. Come on, Mary.'

Kath put her chin in her hands.

'Well?' she demanded.

Her mother picked nervously at a paper tissue in her hand.

'I've to go into hospital for a couple of days,' she said. She took a crumpled piece of paper from her pocket. 'See, here is the letter.'

'Why didn't you say so sooner?' asked Katharine. 'I thought . . .' Gosh, what had she thought? She read

64

the letter. 'What *is* wrong with you? It doesn't say exactly here. Just mentions a minor operation.'

Her mother rubbed under her left arm.

'I have a lump here,' she said. 'The doctor wants it removed at once.'

A slow chill spread through Katharine. She drew her brows together.

'Oh,' she said.

Her mother looked down at the table.

Katharine felt as though she had just stepped off a spinning roundabout. If she stayed very still indeed for a long while everything would be all right again, wouldn't it? Or would it? She could curl herself up into a little ball and pull the covers over her head, as she had done when she was small, and shut her eyes tight, and put her fingers in her ears. She took a deep breath.

'I think,' she said carefully, 'that we will take this very slowly. You are going into hospital tomorrow, and Aunt Betty and I,' she gave a wry smile, 'will cope very well here when you are away. So you will not be concerned for me or the house. And, when you come out, we will manage together, no matter what happens. What do you think of that?'

Her mum smiled at her. Her eyes were full of tears.

'Now,' Katharine stood up. 'I will make some tea.'

Instead of going to the cooker she went round the table, and put her arms round her mother's shoulders, and rubbed her cheek against the side of her face.

'Don't worry,' she whispered, 'it will be all right.'

Her mother dabbed at her eyes with her hankie.

'I don't deserve you, Kath. I should have spoken to you earlier. I'm sorry.'

'I didn't make it easy for you,' mumbled Katharine,

'We are both under pressure, exams and all that. By the way, Hedgehog gave me homework for you to do.'

'Did he? That was considerate of him.'

Katharine grunted as she poured the tea.

'He is thoughtful,' insisted her mother. 'He tries to help me a lot even though he knows I'm a lost cause.'

'You are not a lost cause, Mum,' said Katharine in exasperation. 'You just don't concentrate. You have the ability, I'm sure. It's just that you can't seem to get it together.'

'You can say that again,' said Aunt Betty, as she came into the kitchen.

'You can't seem to get it together' said Katharine obligingly.

Her mother smiled.

'You have my sympathy, Kath,' said Aunt Betty, taking some spaghetti out of a jar and putting it in a pot, 'living with her. She would drive a saint balmy— forgetting things, losing keys, always late. I remember. I was the older sister and I always got the blame. I was expected to look after her all the time.'

Katharine felt quite strange. Here was an unexpected ally in Aunt Betty. Also, her conscience wasn't exactly clear. She should have been aware that her mother was not well. Despite impending exams, she could have helped out a bit more.

She winked at her mother.

'Yes, she is dreadful. I've to practically dress her and put her out to school in the morning.'

Katharine peered into the spaghetti pot.

'Don't you boil the water before you add the spaghetti?' she asked.

'Do you?' said Aunt Betty with interest. 'I'm not a very good cook.'

Katharine could vouch for this. Memories of meals prepared by her aunt filled her mind—lumpy potatoes, greasy chips. She made a face.

Mrs Douglas elbowed them both aside.

'This is one thing I can do,' she said. 'If I am permitted in my own house. You two can set the table.'

They were sitting with coffee and cake in the living-room when Mary called in before going to work.

'Diplomatic relations have been resumed, I gather,' she said cheerfully.

'My sister is the giddy limit,' said Aunt Betty. 'It must be torture for you to have her as a neighbour.'

'Oh, I don't know,' said Mary loyally. 'She helps me with my garden. I weed and water, and buy biological hormone powder, and all my plants die. She comes over and talks to them and they grow.'

She patted Mrs Douglas affectionately on the arm.

'I'll wait behind when I come off duty tomorrow morning and see you admitted into the ward.'

Katharine felt the smile congealing on her face as she waved Mrs McAllister off to work. She had managed to push the fact of her mother's imminent admission to hospital to the back of her mind.

The phone rang as she was preparing for bed. It was Jane.

'Sorry to ring so late, but I was waiting and waiting for you to call me. Is everything OK?'

'Well, I was mistaken in thinking that my mother was going to remarry,' said Katharine. 'She was behaving oddly because she was worried about something.'

Katharine found to her surprise that she could talk quite matter of factly to her friend about her mother's problem. Jane had a very positive attitude.

'Don't worry,' she said. 'My cousin had the exact same thing. She was in and out in two days, no problem. These things are better seen to at once. Have you heard about Louise?'

'No.'

'It's measles.'

'Measles!' shrieked Katharine.

'Absolutely. I phoned her home and spoke to her mum. She's in quarantine for a week. Her mother is having hysterics in case she won't be well enough to sit her exams. Louise is having hysterics in case her face is permanently disfigured. Just think,' said Jane dreamily, 'there is now someone on this planet who has more spots on their face than I have.'

'Poor kid,' said Katharine. 'How embarrassing! Measles!'

'Yes, I told her mum I would let the teachers know tomorrow and they could send her some work home.'

'Tomorrow,' said Katharine, 'I'll be late. I'll go to the hospital first before I come to school.'

'Try not to worry,' said Jane. 'It will be all right. I just know it will.'

TWELVE

There were terrible cramps in Katharine's stomach the next morning as they drove through the hospital gate in Aunt Betty's car. Mrs McAllister was waiting at reception and led them briskly along the corridor to a pleasant little side ward. A nurse was waiting to take down all the personal details.

'Nearest living relative?' she asked.

'Daughter, Katharine,' said Mrs Douglas without hesitation.

Katharine busied herself officiously, turning down the bedclothes, tidying the locker and doing other unnecessary tasks. Her mother changed and got into bed. She seemed very pale and vulnerable against the starched white pillowslips.

'Fine,' said the nurse. 'The consultant will be along this morning and you will probably be seen to later in the day. You can have visitors tonight, but just for a short time,' she added.

Her mother smiled bravely as Katharine kissed her goodbye and gripped her hand tightly.

Aunt Betty dropped Katharine at the school gate. If I hadn't promised to go to school today I would go straight home, thought Katharine. She felt slightly sick. The first person she met was the janitor.

'How's your mother?' he asked.

'Fine,' said Katharine shortly, and hurried on.

Katharine could not concentrate on anything in classes that morning. She kept glancing at her watch, and wondering if her mother had been seen by the doctor, or if she was in theatre. Would she have had anything to eat yet? The morning dragged on. The air became muggy and oppressive.

'I'm going outside,' she said to Jane at lunchtime. 'I don't want anything to eat anyway.'

'I'll bring you a sandwich,' said Jane as she went towards the dinner hall.

Katharine was sitting on the school steps at the front gate when Brian Patterson came up to her.

'I was looking for you,' he said. He cocked his head to one side. 'Are you all right?'

Katherine shrugged her shoulders.

He offered his hand to pull her to her feet.

'Come on,' he said. 'To the art huts. Mrs Wallace wants you to take some of your mum's unfinished sketches home with you. Your mum should be out by the weekend, all being well, and Mrs Wallace is going to ask her to do some work on them. It will be good therapy for her.'

They strolled across to the art huts, together, past groups of other pupils. In ordinary circumstances, Katharine would have swaggered past friends, elated to be seen in such exalted company. Today she could not lift her spirits at all.

'She must have a lot of work at home,' said Mrs Wallace, the art teacher. 'Would you know where it is, Katharine? She was supposed to bring some pieces to me weeks ago but she never did. It is very difficult for me to gather a good selection.'

'She uses our attic as a studio,' said Katharine. 'It's probably all up there, but I don't know if I would know the best things to bring you,' she added doubtfully.

Mrs Wallace tucked some loose strands of hair behind her ears. Katharine watched her. Why did Katharine's own hair falling around her face appear so messy, yet Mrs Wallace could be unkempt and elegant at the same time.

'I could give you a hand,' said Brian.

'What?' Katharine turned to look at him.

'I'm free this weekend. I'll come over on Saturday if you wish, and sort out your mother's paintings, and make a selection. Even if she does get home she may not feel up to it, and it's always good to have another opinion.'

'Would you, Brian?' said Mrs Wallace. 'That's very decent of you. I'm sure Angie would be grateful. Is that suitable, Katharine? It seems such a pity for her not to make a submission at this late stage after all the work she has done. How is her maths doing?'

'I'm going to check with He . . . Mr Hogg later,' said Katharine. 'She will have to do some desperate cramming. Does she need to obtain a good grade for the college?'

'I doubt if they will bother about maths in her case,' said Mrs Wallace. 'She has quite an exceptional talent. A kind of quirky originality, very rare. Makes me rather jealous, in fact. It must have been so frustrating for her—to have that inside her—and be unable to express it for so many years. It is good that she has managed to adjust to her life and start to flower again. I'm sure you are a great asset to her, Katharine. For her to have someone like you beside her, so independent and capable. I'm sure she relies on you a lot.'

Katharine's face was hot. Brian's head was bent over some drawings on the desk, but Katharine was sure he was listening. Did he know how much of this was pleasant fiction imagined by Mrs Wallace?

'I'll go now,' said Katharine. 'Jane was meeting me with a sandwich. I'll see you Saturday, Brian.'

Jane was prancing up and down outside.

'You were seen,' she said. 'It's the talk of the steamie. You were seen actually walking and talking with Number One.'

In her excitement she began eating Katharine's sandwich.

'Excuse me,' said Katharine, and retrieved the sandwich from Jane's fingers. She inspected the mangled bread. 'He only wanted me to sort out Mum's art work,' she said between mouthfuls of crust. 'He is,' she added casually, 'coming over to my house on Saturday to look through her paintings!'

'When?' Jane squealed. 'I'll come and visit you. It is about time you gave The Toad some more help with her homework. I think I'll bring her to your house on Saturday—all day.'

'Don't you dare,' said Katharine. 'It will be embarrassing enough with Aunt Betty bumbling around. I'm going to see if I can find Hedgehog. I want him to give me work my mother can do at home.'

By the time half-past three came, great black clouds were beginning to gather on the horizon. Distant thunder rumbled low and threatening. Kirsty gripped Jane's hand tightly as they hurried down the hill.

'Are you going to the hospital tonight?' asked Jane.

'Uhuh,' said Katharine. 'We're allowed in for a

short time. Will you phone Louise and tell her I was asking for her? I probably won't have time.'

The bus had its lights on as it drew into the stop. It made an eerie sight on a hot afternoon, but the sky was darkening rapidly. Everyone seemed to be in a hurry to be home.

There was no welcoming lamp in the window as Katharine turned the corner at the end of the street, no uplifting smell from the kitchen as she opened the front door. A cold salad lay prepared on the table for her, with a note from Aunt Betty propped up against it.

'Gone for papers and magazines—back soon.'

Katharine sat down wearily and ate some of the food. She gave up after a few moments and took her bag and herself upstairs to change. She had a shower to rid herself of the sticky tension and put on jeans and a sweatshirt. She lay on top of her bed and stared at the ceiling. She began to recite mathematical formulae. She interspersed them with quotes from Macbeth, and threw in some definitions to liven it up.

'Tomorrow and tomorrow and tomorrow creeps in this petty pace from day to day.'

He had said it all, she thought. William S. She heard Aunt Betty coming. Hospital time. Pin your smile on. Rehearse the platitudes. 'You're looking great'. Did adults ever mean those things they said? She would probably end up doing it herself. If I do, she thought, I'll jump in the river on the way home.

Aunt Betty was extremely nervous driving the car. Her fingers clenched the wheel tightly and she sat hunched up in her seat.

'It's going to be a bad night,' she said. 'Look at those clouds. It's so dark.'

It was dark, unnaturally dark. Strange blue lightning flickered in the belly of the clouds as they moved sullenly in the sky.

Her mother lay quiet and alone in the little room where they had left her that morning. Nothing had changed and yet everything had changed. The lump had been removed, they would see how well she healed, and then . . . The die was cast. The room did not seem to belong to her any more, Katharine decided. She belonged to it. The disinfectant smell had taken over. It was through her clothes, in her hair, on her skin.

'Does it hurt?' asked Katharine.

'Not much, truthfully. Don't look like that, Katharine. They are very nice here. The nurses are wonderful. So kind and patient. Now there's a woman in the main ward who . . .'

Her mother and Aunt Betty began to discuss ailments and conditions which Katharine never knew existed, had not thought possible, and, what was more, did not want to know anything about, she decided.

After a minute or two the ward sister came in.

'I'm going to chase you,' she said. 'Your mum is doing very well. We are very pleased with her. She will see the doctor tomorrow and should get out for the weekend. There's no reason why she cannot go home, provided she has rested.'

'Well, we'll take our cue from that,' said Aunt Betty.

She got up and kissed her sister.

'I'll come tomorrow,' she said.

Katharine hugged her mum.

'Oh, I forgot to tell you,' she said. 'Mrs Wallace was looking for some more of your work. So Brian offered to come round on Saturday and help sort out your paintings. She has also given me some sketches which she wants you to finish. And Hedgehog, sorry, Mr Hogg has sent work too.'

'Heavens,' said her mother. 'No rest for the wicked. I'll do the drawings. I don't know about the maths. I was thinking of giving the exam a miss.'

'What?' said Katharine. 'After all that effort. You must be joking. We'll talk about it later,' she added hurriedly as she saw how tired her mother appeared.

'Oh, and the Janny sends his warmest regards. So you had better hurry up and be well. He has got you down as number one candidate for mothering his two brats.'

'Heaven forbid,' her mother laughed.

Katharine gave her a quick hug.

'See you tomorrow,' she whispered.

Aunt Betty turned from the window as Katharine came out of the ward.

'Look at this,' she said.

From high on the hill where they were they could see down the valley. A spectacular view on a clear day, tonight they were watching a tremendous electrical storm sweeping over from the hills. The lightning crackled blue and white, great jagged forks illuminating the trees and houses. A great crack of thunder followed at once, seemingly directly above their heads. The lights in the hospital flickered and stayed on. Aunt Betty turned the collar of her jacket up.

'Come on,' she said. 'Let's get home as fast as possible.'

Later in bed, Katharine could not sleep. She opened the window. The air was still oppressive, heavy and still. The world waited. And then she heard the first drops of rain spat out of the sky. She got up and pulled on a track suit over her pyjamas. She let herself quietly out of the back door into the garden. The earth, dry after weeks of sun, welcomed the rain. So did Katharine. She lifted her face to the sky as it poured down. She lifted her arms to the sky as the water flattened her hair to her scalp and soaked through her clothes. Tears mingled with the rain on her face.

THIRTEEN

'I rang the hospital,' said Aunt Betty as she was making toast the next morning. 'They say your mum had a good night despite the storm.'

She looked at Katharine more closely.

'Did you sleep well? You look tired.'

'Not too badly,' said Katharine. She decided not to mention her midnight wanderings in the garden. 'I had a strange dream, all mixed up. I was swimming in the sea and the shore kept moving further away. I hate it when you wake up in the middle of a dream.'

Aunt Betty patted her hand as she put tea and toast in front of her.

'Not to worry,' she said reassuringly. 'I'm sure if you analysed it, it's a perfectly normal dream to have under the circumstances. Eat up your breakfast and get away to school. I'll meet you at three-thirty with the car and we'll get some groceries for the weekend.'

Malcolm was coming out of his front gate as Katharine left her house and he fell into step beside her. The pavement was steaming quietly as the sun started to dry out last night's heavy rain. The grass and the trees were new-washed green as if from a child's colouring book.

'That was some storm last night,' said Malcolm. 'A cracker. I was watching it from my bedroom window. Spectacular. The dog went mad, hiding under my bed, whining.'

'Poor thing,' said Katharine. 'I find storms exciting, scary but exciting.'

'Yes, I noticed,' said Malcolm. 'Having a midnight stroll? There are simpler ways of washing your hair, you know.'

Katharine laughed. 'I had to get out. It was so stuffy. I needed air and time to think.'

'How is your mum?' asked Malcolm.

'Fine so far. She was a bit subdued last night.'

'And how is Aunt Betty?'

'Not too bad, if the truth be told,' said Katharine. 'She seems to have improved, or perhaps it's because Meg isn't with her.'

'Oh, I remember Meg,' said Malcolm, 'the sneak. She was the reason my pocket money was stopped for several weeks, by helping my dad establish the identity of the person who broke three windows in our greenhouse. Come on, there's the bus.'

Katharine went straight to the school office when she arrived. She collected work from Mr Hogg for her mother to do. He explained to her what he wanted done.

'Try to be patient, Katharine, when your mother asks you something.'

'Yes, yes,' said Katharine. At least she wasn't as sarcastic as he was, or downright sadistic like Mr Jack.

As she was leaving she bumped into Mrs Wallace. 'The very person I'm looking for. I've just had

Louise's mother on the phone. She will be unable to model for the Art Exam. Katharine, would you do it for me, dear? You have such a strong profile, and I'm sure you will be able to keep still. You must have modelled for your mother dozens of times. Thanks very much, you are a pet. Monday morning, 9 am, studio two in the art huts. I will write a note to your class teacher to excuse you for a block.' She hurried off.

Katharine nearly dropped the papers she was holding.

'But . . . but . . .' It was too late. Mrs Wallace was gone.

'I think I am the teacher in question,' said Mr Hogg who had been standing smirking, watching her. I certainly think you can spare the time away, but I will give you extra homework at the weekend to compensate!'

Katharine made a face at his retreating back.

'I don't want to do it,' she said to Jane later. 'Last week, yes, in fact, I was quite jealous of Louise, but not now.'

'Don't be silly. You are feeling low, because of your mum and everything. This is just what you need to cheer you up.' She went on as Katharine remained unconvinced. 'It will be good for your mum. When she comes home from hospital at the weekend she can help you choose what to wear. It will take her mind off her own problems for a bit. She can do your make-up, fix your hair . . .' she trailed off.

'My hair!' shrieked Katharine. 'I'd forgotten about that. No, definitely not, I'm not doing it.'

'You and your hair,' said Jane. 'I'm fed up hearing about your hair. It's not as bad as you think it is.

Anyway you could put on a hat, tie a scarf on it, wind a turban round it.'

'Put a sock in it,' said Katharine nastily.

'Look,' said Jane seriously. 'I've been making allowances for you, but don't push your luck, kiddo.'

'Sorry,' said Katharine. 'I think I'll go to the library and do some work. I would be better on my own just now.'

After school she chatted more calmly with Jane at the main gate as she waited for her aunt.

'Where *is* Kirsty?' Jane glanced anxiously down the road. 'She's usually here before us.'

A small figure appeared behind a mass of greenery.

'I brought these for your mum,' said Kirsty, ''cos she is in hospital.'

Bunches of great red-headed rhododendrons, and bright purple lilac were mixed with branches of evergreen.

'They are beautiful, darling,' said Katharine.

'Where did you get them?' said Jane at once.

'I'll tell you exactly where she got them.' An irate janitor appeared from the school gates. 'My garden, that's where.' He grabbed Kirsty by the ear. 'And you are going to put them right back.'

Kirsty howled.

'Just a minute,' said Katharine. 'She didn't know it was your garden. Did you, pet? There, you see,' she went on, without waiting for an answer. 'Here, you can have them back.'

She turned to Kirsty.

'Those flowers are too ordinary for my mum. Why don't you bring her something from your garden? It's only special things that grow there. There, there. Never mind.' She wiped the tears away from Kirsty's eyes. 'Never mind this nasty man. It was a nice thought for you to have, to gather flowers for a poor sick lady in hospital.'

Kirsty sniffed.

Aunt Betty drove up at this moment. She got out of her car.

'What is going on?' she asked.

'I didn't know,' said the janitor. 'If I had known the flowers were for Mrs Douglas. If the little girl had said . . .' he protested.

'Come on,' said Aunt Betty. 'I'll give your friend a lift home.'

When they were all safely in the car, Aunt Betty asked, 'What was that all about?'

'Nothing,' said three voices in unison.

'Did you make a list?' asked Katharine as they selected a trolley and started up the first aisle of the supermarket.

'Here it is.'

Katharine took a pen from her pocket and began to number the items.

'What are you doing?' Aunt Betty peered over her shoulder.

'I am putting them in the correct sequence,' said Katharine. 'I would have thought that was obvious. It saves so much time.' She took a firm hold of her aunt's arm. 'This way.'

'Well, Katharine,' said Aunt Betty at the check-out, twenty minutes later. 'I am truly amazed. This is the fastest I have ever shopped in my life, but then I have never shopped with a person who arranges their shopping list in the exact order in which the goods are laid out in their supermarket. I don't know whether to be scared or impressed.'

'Why?' asked Katharine. 'It saves all that dithering about.'

'This may come as a shock to you, Katharine,' said Aunt Betty with a trace of amusement in her voice, 'some people actually like dithering about.'

Over dinner, Katharine laid out Mr Hogg's maths notes and studied them as she ate.

'Homework, dear?' asked Aunt Betty, as she cleared up.

'Yes, but not for me. It's for Mum. She is going to pass this maths exam, I have decided. Here is the plan. After visiting tonight I will wait on and give her some tuition. Malcolm's dad takes Mrs McAllister to work on a Friday night. He will collect me when he does that tonight and bring me home.'

'Do you think your mother is up to it?' asked her aunt doubtfully.

'It will take her mind off her tests. If she is too tired I'll stop. But I think if she thinks she might get through the exam it will give her the lift she needs right now.'

Mrs Douglas laughed out loud at Betty's story.

'Oh, yes, Katharine has always been like that. It is quite an experience shopping with her: no dallying, you are not allowed to buy anything which is not on the list, and she always knows exactly what the bill should be.'

Katharine was inspecting her mother's cards.

'You nearly had half the Janny's garden in here tonight,' she said. 'The Toad uprooted tons of his best plants. You should have seen him. He was furious.'

'So that was what was going on this afternoon,' said Aunt Betty. 'The poor man. The way you were haranguing him, Katharine, one would have thought he was the criminal.'

Mrs Douglas's eyes travelled towards the door.

'My gosh,' she said. She sat up in bed and started to straighten the covers. 'Look who's here.'

Katharine, turned towards the door. A rather embarrassed Mr Hogg stood clutching a bunch of flowers. He hovered at the door.

'Come in,' said Katharine in a loud voice. 'Do.' She moved up to make room for him.

'Just thought I'd pop in as I was passing,' he said nervously. 'I brought you these.' He shoved the flowers at Katharine's mother.

'Really? Do you come all the way into town past the hospital,' asked Katharine innocently. She was enjoying this.

Aunt Betty stood up.

'Visiting time is nearly over,' she said. 'I'm going. Katharine is staying on tonight. Something about some maths tuition,' she smiled. 'However,' she hauled on Katharine's arm, 'she is walking me out to the car. Aren't you, dear?'

'You spoiled that for me,' grumbled Katharine as they went along the corridor. 'I could have had some fun there.'

'That was very obvious. But I don't know if your mum would have enjoyed it. I'll see you later.'

Katharine hung about outside until she spotted Hedgehog leaving. Her mother's face was quite pink when she returned to the room.

'I'll soon wipe that smile from your face,' said Katharine as she dumped the maths books on the bed.

'I was thinking, dear, that I would do the exam next year.'

'Yes,' said Katharine, 'and I am thinking that you will do it this year.' She opened a book. 'After all, we can't let teacher be disappointed.

'Quadratic equations. See where you have written this? If you start at the top and follow the sequence through you will see where you have gone wrong.'

'I will?' said her mother.

'Yes,' said Katharine firmly. 'You can't do what you have written here.'

'Why not?'

'It is not logical,' said Katharine.

'Oh, Katharine,' her mother laughed. 'You sound like Spock in Star Trek.'

'Look,' said Katharine in desperation. 'You appreciate poetry, don't you. Well, think of these as a poem. It has a pattern, a rhythm, a natural sequence. Let's start again.'

'I'll say this,' said Mrs Douglas after an hour. 'I don't know if I have learned anything, but it is the first time that I have actually enjoyed a maths lesson.'

Katharine felt very pleased with herself. She reminded her mother about Brian Patterson coming round the following day.

'You will get home won't you?'

'I'm sure of it,' said her mother. 'I'm healing up nicely.' Her face clouded. 'Then it's a case of monthly check-ups, and hopefully no further problems. Don't worry,' she added, seeing Katharine's expression, 'I won't skip any appointments.'

Katharine gathered up the books.

'I'll leave this one in case you're bored, or can't sleep tonight.'

She went to the Premature Baby unit to meet Mrs McAllister.

'How is she?' asked Mrs McAllister.

'A lot better,' said Katharine.

'I'll take my tea with her later. Come and see my babies.'

She put a mask on Katharine.

'Look at this wee toe rag,' she said. 'Two days old and weighing less than a bag of sugar.'

Katharine looked at the tiny baby through the glass.

'Will it survive?' she asked.

'Of course, she'll survive,' said Malcolm's mother. 'She's got me on her side.'

She walked further on.

'Look. This one's called Wallace,' she said. 'He's been very ill, but he's a bonny fighter, just like his namesake.'

The little baby was waving his arms and legs about.

'Your dad used to come here a lot. He was doing valuable research on infant mortality.' She sighed. 'He was a lovely man. You are very like him, Katharine. He was passionately fond of living things.'

So her father had been a conservationist, thought Katharine, as she lay in bed that night, listening to the wind in the trees. She could remember snatches of things from her childhood. Days on the beach, a picnic in the Campsie Hills. Little pieces of a life to fit together. But there would always be big gaps. She could never complete that picture. A terrible sadness took hold of her. She thought of her mother in the hospital alone. Was it worse for her because she had known him longer, or better because she had more memories. She didn't know. It was only after people had died that you saw how much you cared. And now her own mother's life might be in jeopardy. She wasn't a child. She couldn't pretend it wasn't happening, and hope that the problem would go away.

FOURTEEN

The next morning Aunt Betty and Katharine rushed around the house cleaning and tidying. Katharine changed her mother's bed and arranged some flowers in a tall glass on her bedside table—pink and white honeysuckle that was just beginning to bloom. Their poignant smell filled the room.

Soon it was time to leave for the hospital.

'Are you going dressed like that?' asked Aunt Betty.

'Why not?' Katharine was wearing long safari shorts and a T-shirt.

Her aunt shrugged. 'Oh, I don't know. Come on, let's go.'

Her mother was packed and waiting when they arrived.

'She has been this way since seven o'clock this morning,' said the ward sister.

'I feel as though I've been away for ages,' said Mrs Douglas as she came into her house. 'Gosh, everything is so tidy, Betty. You must have been working hard.'

'Kath did most of it,' said Aunt Betty loyally. 'She has made your room very pretty. Now, we will have some lunch and then you can go for a lie down.'

* * *

With her mother resting and Aunt Betty reading downstairs, Katharine tried to concentrate on some studying. She would try an English past paper. She struggled through the interpretation. Where did they pick these passages from, she wondered? This one dealt with urbanisation following the industrial revolution, walking for pleasure, the development of the Girl Guide and Boy Scout movement. Riveting stuff. Katharine lifted her head. Birds were whistling. She could hear the voices of children playing in the garden further down the street. The world was beckoning her. She bent over her work.

The doorbell rang.

Aunt Betty called up the stairs.

'Someone to see you, Katharine. A boy,' she added in a significant tone.

Brian! Katharine smoothed her hair down as best she could.

'Mum is lying down,' she told him as they went up the little stairs to the attic. 'We could collect some things and show them to her when she wakes up.'

Long rays of afternoon sun filled the small room.

'I can see why she paints up here,' said Brian. 'The light is magnificent. The whole room is throbbing with it. And nothing but sky above.'

He moved around the room, gazing at drawings and paintings that were pinned to the wall or lying on the floor.

'A lot of this stuff is unfinished.'

'I'm not surprised,' said Katharine, 'with what she had on her mind.'

'How is she?'

'We won't know the results of the test until next week. She's certainly looking a lot better. She seems in better spirits too. As if she is relieved that it's all out in the open.'

She went over to the table in the middle of the room. There were tubes of paint and pots of cleaning fluid, brushes and bottles of linseed oil. Katharine poked among these.

'Could you get high on any of these?' she asked.

'Would you want to?' asked Brian.

'I was thinking you could mix me a special potion to help me pass the "O" Grades.'

'If I could do that I would patent it and become a millionaire,' he laughed. 'There is no substitute for hard work, my girl.'

He started to look at a pile of canvases stacked against the far wall.

'These are all completed,' he said.

Katharine joined him.

'I think these are older ones. Yes, that's where we used to live.'

She knelt down beside him.

'I can remember this vaguely.'

It was a pen and ink sketch of a tenement back court.

'I used to play down there.'

Two women were standing on the drying green. One, her mouth full of pegs, was hanging out washing. The other had a baby on her hip.

'Her art is so full of life,' said Brian.

Katharine pulled out another. It showed a park. Flower beds were set out in formal lines, rows of tall ivory lily tulips set among clumps of burgundy wall-flowers. The effect was stunning.

Katharine sat back on her heels.

'This is you, isn't it?' Brian extracted a watercolour

from the pile. The painting showed a young child asleep under a tree. Golden hair made a soft frame around her face.

Katharine examined it.

'Yes. Now, that one I don't remember. It's from way back. It's only in the last year that Mum has started painting again.' She thought for a minute. 'It must have been frustrating for her. To have all that talent burning inside and not be able to express it. Actually, you can tell it's an old picture. Look at the colour of my hair. That's before it developed into this.' She pulled at a clump of her hair.

'What's wrong with it?' asked Brian.

'Condition? Texture? Colour? Pick any or all.'

'Colour? What's wrong with the colour?'

'Red,' said Katharine. 'Beetroot, lobster, carrot, ginger, orange, tomato.'

'They're all food, Katharine,' said Brian. 'That's very Freudian.'

He took a strand of her hair in his own fingers.

'Copper,' he said. 'Old gold, russet, amber, ochre, burnt sienna, flame, titian.' He rolled the words on his tongue.

'Come on,' said Katharine.

Brian shook his head. He spread her hair across her hand.

'Look at the light in it. It's on fire. Red is the colour of the sun, the symbol of life. A matador's cloak, a heart.'

'Goodness,' said Katharine feeling uncomfortable. 'You're not into poetry by any chance? One of Mrs Travers's chums?'

'Alas, no,' said Brian. He let the strands of hair fall

one by one. He looked into her face. 'But I can appreciate beauty when I see it.'

Katharine's throat went tight. A very odd feeling was growing in her stomach.

'Well, you're not going to get the chance to appreciate it much during your exam. Louise has the measles.'

'Louise?' he said blankly.

'Yes,' gabbled Katharine. 'The pretty one, blonde, blue eyes. My mum says she looks like a Botticelli angel.'

'Oh, *Louise*. Yes she is very pretty.'

Katharine's heart dropped.

He leaned towards her.

'I prefer faces with character.'

With his finger he traced the line of her eyebrow, down her nose, round the side of her mouth and came to rest just under her bottom lip. He pressed very gently.

Katharine stayed very still. The dust motes danced in the sunlight. The room was very quiet. He smiled. His eyes are very dark she thought, black, dark eyes.

He took his hand away and sat back on his heels.

'I'm choosing this one anyway,' he said, placing the painting of her as a child to one side against the wall.

Katharine started breathing again. She stood up carefully, balancing herself against the wall.

'I'll choose the drawing of the back court,' she said, and put them together.

The door opened and her mother came in.

'I thought I heard voices,' she said. 'How are you managing? A lot of dross in there, Brian.'

'And some little nuggets as well,' said Brian. He

stood up. 'None of your work is dross, it's all worth-while. What do you think of the ones we've selected? They are representative of your many skills. If you finish those Mrs Wallace has sent you I think that will do.'

'Good,' said Mrs Douglas. 'I'll take your word for it. I came to tell you that Aunt Betty is making some food, if you would like to come down.'

'Oh, no,' said Katharine 'You should have told her I would make the tea. This smells like cremated pig.'

'Bacon sandwiches, everyone?' asked Aunt Betty brightly, as they came into the kitchen.

'Certainly,' said Brian gazing at the bacon on the table. 'Only, may I have mine without the bacon, please?'

Katharine giggled.

Aunt Betty looked at the plate sadly.

'You are quite wise, Brian,' she said. She scraped the food into the bin. 'I'll put together some salad for you.'

'A coffee will do me,' said Brian. 'I have to go home for dinner tonight.'

Katharine walked him to the gate.

'See you on Monday,' she said. 'I'm going to ask my mother what I should wear, so don't freak out when you see me.'

He rested his elbows on the gate.

'I won't,' he promised. 'What type of clothes do you like to wear?'

'Casual,' said Katharine. 'What I'm wearing now.' She indicated her shorts and shirt.'

'Mmmm,' he said. 'What would you wear, for instance, to the end-of-term disco?'

'Don't know. I'll probably be allowed something new.'

'So, you *are* going to the disco?'

'Yes.'

'With anyone in particular?'

Katharine's heart began to beat very slowly.

'Ah,' she said, hesitating.

'I'm not surprised,' said Brian.

'Jane and Louise and I agreed to go together,' said Katharine. 'I don't want to go back on my word.'

'Very commendable,' he said lightly. He took her wrist. 'Would you pencil me in for a dance in your dance card, here?'

'Certainly, sir.' Katharine pretended to inscribe his name in a booklet attached to her wrist. 'Baron Brian,' she said. 'The Polka.'

He touched her lightly on the cheek.

'Make it the last dance, would you?' He walked away.

Katharine leaned weakly on the gate and watched him until he was out of sight, sauntering down the street, hands in pockets.

I must phone Jane she thought, and Louise. She returned to the kitchen.

'Katharine, dear. You look quite flushed. You're not sickening for something, I hope,' said her mother. 'Oh dear, not with the exams coming up.' She placed her hand on Katharine's forehead.

'I've never felt better in my life,' said Katharine. She started whistling as she set the table. 'I have something to tell you. I was saving it until you came home. You know that Louise has measles. Well, Mrs Wallace has asked me to take her place on Monday. So rack your brains and decide how I am to appear. This one is going to take all of your many skills.'

FIFTEEN

Katharine watched her aunt and mother embrace at the front door. Aunt Betty stroked her mother's hair.

'I'm sorry I can't stay longer, but Kath is more than able to look after you. Remember and phone as soon as you hear. Good luck in the exams, Katharine. You'll probably eat them. I'll go home now and lean on Meg, and try to get her to open a book for a few hours.'

'It was good of you to come,' said Mrs Douglas.

'It was nothing. Kath is perfectly capable of seeing to herself. She needs you to let her grow up.'

She eased herself into her car.

'Bye.'

'Aunt Betty and Mrs McAllister told me that you'd known about that lump weeks before you went to the doctor,' said Katharine to her mother as they re-entered the house.

'Did they?' said her mother evasively.

'Well, that was just silly,' said Katharine. 'If it isn't malignant then there's nothing to worry about. If it is, then the sooner seen to the better. A lot of these things are curable.'

'You are remarkably well-informed.'

'We have talks in Guidance and Health Education

Classes. You must promise me never to neglect anything like that again.'

'I promise. Now, shall we investigate the possibility of turning you into the Mona Lisa?'

'It's irrelevant what I wear,' said Katharine disconsolately after an hour of searching through her mother's and her own wardrobe. Mounds of clothes lay on the bed, on the floor and in the chest of drawers. She wandered over to the mirror.

'It all comes back to the same thing,' she said. 'This mop.' She shook her head until her hair came loose. 'A woman's crowning glory.' She sat down on the end of the bed. 'I hate it. It's the bane of my life.' She rubbed her hands furiously on her head. Her hair stood out with static electricity. 'I look like "Oor Wullie",' she said, 'or "Worzel Gummidge". Or even the scarecrow in "The Wizard of Oz".' She was close to tears.

'I had no idea that you felt it such a problem,' said her mother. 'You never said to me. Why don't you have it cut short?'

'I don't want it short,' wailed Katharine. 'Besides, it's only the weight of it which keeps it in order.'

'That's not strictly true,' said her mother. 'Perhaps for the back but not the front. If you had that cut it would give it a bit more freedom.'

'A bit more freedom,' cried Katharine. 'If I gave it any freedom it would escape altogether.'

Her mother laughed.

'You make it sound like a desperate maniac.'

'It is,' muttered Katharine darkly. 'It's ruining my life.'

'Here, let me try something.' Her mother sat her in a chair. She combed the front half of Katharine's hair forward, and made a parting across the top of her head from ear to ear. Then she deftly corn-plaited the back section. She swung Katharine round to look.

'There, neat and attractive, and the length and weight at the back will hold it in place. Now for the front.' She picked up a pair of scissors.

'I hope you know what you're doing,' said Katharine.

'So do I,' whispered her mum.

She snipped and talked as she worked.

'Your hair has a natural curl in it. You have to do something with it. Perhaps tong it into shape. Help the natural life of the hair express itself. That should appeal to you Katharine.'

'You're really enjoying yourself, aren't you?' asked Katharine.

'It makes me feel good when I am creating something. I feel alive.'

'There is something I would like to ask you,' said Katharine. 'It's personal,' she added awkwardly.

'Go ahead.' Her mother was standing in front of her, twisting strands of hair round her little finger and gently teasing them into ringlet shapes.

'How did Dad and you get on? Everyone says he was like me, and we're such opposites.'

Her mother thought for a minute, and then looked Katharine straight in the eyes.

'We were in love,' she said simply.

'This reminds me of rag ringlets my mum used to put in my hair,' her mother went on, 'when I was small. She took strips of cloth and curled the sections of wet hair down the whole length, round and round, and then tied them up at the end. You were sent out to play with them in. They often stayed in all night.

96

That's why my hair stayed curly without the aid of mousse or gels.'

She held a mirror in front of Katharine.

'What do you think?'

Tiny curls and wisps of hair framed Katharine's face at the front. The rest was pulled back severely into the plait which started at the crown and, drawing hair from the sides, rested on the back of her neck.

'That's really nice,' said Katharine in some surprise. She resembled the young girl in the painting in the attic.

'I'm not finished. That would do for every day. What we want for Monday is something more spectacular.' She began undoing the plait.

'What have you got in mind?' asked Katharine nervously.

'Mmmm.' Her mother switched on the hot curling brush.

'Don't look in the mirror until I'm finished.'

She began to curl Katharine's hair, section upon section, tight curls which she then brushed out firmly.

'This is going to be flamboyant,' said Katharine.

'Yes.'

'I'm not going to like it.'

'Be quiet, if you don't have the nerve to go through with it then we can plait it again.' She stood back and surveyed her handiwork. 'You're going to knock 'em dead,' she said.

'Hang on a second.' She pulled a white, plain, draped dress from a hanger. 'This was a maxi dress, years ago when the maxis were in first time around.'

She helped Katharine into the dress. She cleared the small bedside table which had a long tablecloth and placed it in front of the mirror. She gave Katharine a spray of honeysuckle to hold.

'Imagine that this is an arum lily,' she said, 'hold it so.'

She laid the flower across Katharine's arm.

'As if you are carrying a baby. Now go and stand beside the table and look in the mirror.'

'Gosh,' said Katharine.

'I couldn't have put it better myself.'

Katharine gazed at the glass.

'Is that me?'

'*Beata Katerina*,' her mother said softly. There were tears in her eyes.

'What?'

'You remind me of a Pre-Raphaelite painting. Except that you are more striking.'

'I don't know about this,' said Katharine. She twisted round to see herself at the back. 'It's a bit revealing here.'

'We'll put a pin in it. Will you wear it?'

Katharine took a deep breath.

'Yes,' she said.

'I'll go to the florists first thing in the morning, and buy an arum lily.'

'Don't be ridiculous,' said Katharine. 'An artificial flower would do.'

'Oh, no. It has to be the genuine article. There's nothing phoney about you, Katharine.'

Katharine walked closer to the mirror.

'You can see my freckles,' she said.

'The sun's brought them out. We'll apply some cover make-up.'

Katharine tossed her head.

'No. I've decided I like them.' She pulled at a curl of hair on her forehead. It sprang back into place.

'It is incredible,' she said. 'Do you think it will stay this way?'

'No. You'll have to use conditioner, and the hot brush or rollers. Or perhaps a perm. A soft one,' she added as she saw Katharine's face. 'You get undressed and I'll make some dinner, and then we'd both better do some studying.'

Katharine took one last look in the mirror.

'It's such a simple outfit, yet so striking.'

'Was it Michelangelo who said "take infinite pains to make something that looks effortless"?'

'Good grief!' said Katharine. 'I don't know. I haven't caught up with Macbeth yet.'

SIXTEEN

Something was different, thought Katharine. She rolled over in bed and woke up. She put her hand to her head. Her hair. She got up and looked in the mirror. It seemed to her as though she had lost an awful lot of it, and what was left was behaving badly in protest.

'Mum,' she wailed.

Her mother appeared at the bedroom door.

'My hair has taken a fit.'

'Don't be silly. Go and have a shower, and I'll fix it for you. For heaven's sake!'

'I don't know if I can go through with this,' muttered Katharine as she stuffed the white dress into a plastic carrier bag.

'You can and you will,' said her mother taking the dress back out and folding it carefully. 'The exam won't start until half-past nine, by which time I'll have arrived with the lily. I'll give your hair a good brush out. Honestly, Kath, the way you go on you would think that your hair had a character of its own.'

'It has,' said Katharine, 'and it's an evil one.'

Her mother laughed and pushed her out the door to school.

'See you later.'

'What have you done to your hair,' said Jane when they met in the cloakroom.

'It's what my mother has done,' said Katharine. 'Helped by a pair of scissors. What do you think. Is it OTT?'

'I can hardly see it,' said Jane. 'The way you have your neck sunk into your chin, and your blazer collar turned up doesn't help.'

She walked slowly round Katharine.

'It's good,' she said slowly. 'Different but dramatic, daring and dynamic, definitely dashing despite—'

Katharine pushed Jane away.

Phyllis Calgary was leaning on a coat peg.

'What is orange and sounds like a parrot?' she asked of no one in particular.

'Carrot,' said Katharine at once. 'What is nasty and rhymes with witch?'

'Phyllis?' suggested Jane.

The bell rang.

'Don't leave me!' screamed Katharine.

Jane prised her friend's fingers from her wrist.

'Screw your courage to the sticking place,' she said. And as Katharine hesitated. 'Go on,' she urged. 'Beat it, scram.'

Katharine tried to walk as nonchalantly as possible across the playground to the art huts. She met a couple of the Sixth Years on the way.

'Are you the model?' asked Stuart Cunningham. 'What have you got in the plastic bag? A topless swimsuit, I hope.'

'Shut up, Stuart,' the School Captain, a girl called Maureen said. 'That's a sexist remark. I'll report you to the First Year Feminist Group and have you neutered. Just ignore him,' she said to Katharine. 'His hormones are giving him bother. Boys take much longer to mature than girls do.'

She showed Katharine into a small room next door to the studio in which the exam was to take place.

'You can get changed in here,' she said. 'Mrs Wallace should be along to see you in ten minutes or so.'

Katharine struggled into the dress. Her mother had applied stocking cream to her legs as she was supposed to be barefoot. Katharine was beginning to have serious doubts about the wisdom of the venture. She went to work on her hair, curling it round her fingers as she had watched her mother do. The door opened.

'Sorry I'm late,' said her mother. 'I have a very good reason for once. I had to wait for the florist opening. But it was worth it. Look.'

She unwrapped the tissue paper from the object she was carrying and showed Katharine a beautiful white arum lily. The funnel of the flower curved back gently revealing a dusting of yellow inside.

'It's perfect,' breathed Katharine.

'Here you are then.'

'What about my hair?' asked Katharine.

'It's lovely,' said her mother. She flounced it out more at the sides with her hands. 'Now whatever you do, don't smile. Aim for the bored and sultry look.'

Mrs Wallace came in.

'Are you ready, Katharine?'

'As I'll ever be. Lead on, MacDuff.'

'That is incorrect, Katharine,' said Mrs Wallace crisply. 'A line from Macbeth often misquoted. The phrase is in fact, "*Lay* on, MacDuff". You had better do some more English revision before the exam. Come along.'

Katharine made a face to her mother behind Mrs Wallace's back as she followed her out of the room.

'Let me have a good look at you,' said Mrs Wallace just before they entered the studio. 'Mmmm, the lily is excellent. And you, Katharine, dear, are stunning. Now what would be a good pose?'

'My mum thought perhaps I could lean my elbow on a table.'

Katharine slouched her shoulders and slumped over an imaginary table.

'I hardly think your mother pictured you quite like that,' said Mrs Wallace. 'But I can see what she means. Posing languidly in deep reflective thought. OK we have props which will help.' She opened the Art Room door and ushered Katharine in. '"Lead on, brave heart",' she said, '"and I will follow after." And if you don't recognise that quote, Katharine, you may look it up, but it is not from Macbeth.'

Katharine gripped her lily tightly and sidled into the room.

'Kath?' said Brian.

'Gosh,' said Stuart. He dropped his pencil, bent to pick it up, straightened and bumped his head on his easel.

Mrs Wallace busied herself about Katharine, adjusting the folds of the dress, placing and replacing the lily.

'I think it would be better if you stood,' she said. She tilted Katharine's chin. 'Gaze into the middle distance and think deep thoughts. What you intend to have for lunch, for instance.'

* * *

'It was really boring,' Katharine told Jane later.

'Boring,' said Jane. 'Boring. The chance of a life-time to impress the best talent in Sixth Year, and you tell me it was boring.'

'Honestly, Jane,' said Katharine. 'My nose got itchy, my feet ached, my back was sore, and I was thoroughly sick of the whole thing. If I moved a fraction of an inch, everyone tutted. It was awful.'

They were walking slowly down the hill from the school. Kirsty skipped ahead of them.

'Louise didn't miss a thing. I'm going to see her on my way home. Are you coming? It's all right,' she added as Jane nodded towards Kirsty. 'She's no longer infectious.'

They sat on the end of Louise's bed while her mother fussed round.

'Most important of all,' said Jane. 'Here is the school work which you have to do.' She laid a pile of notes on the dressing table. 'That will keep you out of mischief for a while.'

Katharine patted her friend on the arm. 'Honestly, Louise,' she said. 'Don't be terribly disappointed about the art exam. It was deadly dull. Would I lie?'

'Yes,' said Louise, 'but thanks anyway. Toady,' she said to Jane's young sister, 'don't get the measles whatever you do.'

'I've had them,' said Kirsty. 'Look, I've brung you some flowers.'

'Oh, no,' said Katharine and Jane in unison.

But Kirsty only presented Louise with a few dandelions and a cluster of dock leaves.

'When shall we three meet again?' said Louise miserably.   *   *   *

'Oh, be quiet,' said Jane. 'If I hear another Shakespeare quote, I'll kill myself.'

Katharine got off the bus at the end of the road and swung her schoolbag on to her shoulder. The bag containing the dress was crushed somewhere near the bottom. It seemed such a long time ago. All these trivial things which had worried her—exams looming ahead, the end of term disco—had been put into perspective. She smiled to herself. She was beginning to think in artistic terms.

The lamp her mother always kept on, winter or summer, glowed in the window. A welcoming light for her to focus on. She quickened her pace along the street towards her home.

SEVENTEEN

'I feel sick,' said Jane. Her teeth were chattering as she leaned over the sink in the school cloakroom.

'No you don't.' Katharine patted her friend on the back. 'It's just nerves. Remember Einstein never passed a maths exam in his life. Here, have a drink of water. How are you doing, Louise?'

Louise was propped up against the mirror. She brushed her hair absently.

'After that English "O" Grade, I'm past caring. I'm convinced that I wrote that it was Duncan who murdered Macbeth. And what's more I've used quotes to prove it.' She giggled. 'I think I'm going hysterical. The invigilator kept pacing up and down beside my desk.'

'You were very pale,' said Katharine. 'Perhaps she thought you were going to faint.'

'I would have done, if I thought it might help. I feel a lot better today. I could hold my breath until I passed out, and then maybe they would send me home.' She breathed in and held her breath until her face became bright red.

'Stop, for heaven's sake,' said Katharine. 'You're beginning to worry me.'

Jane started laughing.

'Well, at any rate, you've cheered her up.'

'No, she hasn't,' groaned Jane, clutching her stomach. 'She's making me worse.'

'Let's go for a walk outside,' suggested Katharine. 'We have half an hour to spare.' She linked arms with her friends and they went towards the main doors.

'It's much too nice to be sitting exams,' complained Louise, as they sauntered round the yard.

Jane took deep breaths.

'That was a good idea. I'm beginning to come to.'

'Well, just look what the two of you have done to me.' Katharine held out her hands. They were trembling slightly.

'Thank goodness for that,' said Louise. 'I was beginning to doubt if you were human.'

They strolled along the front of the school. Other pupils had had the same idea. Groups of friends stood or sat on the grass, chatting, some desperately leafing through text books.

They looked down into the art studios. All was quiet and empty.

'Did your mum manage to complete her folio?' asked Jane.

'Yes, the College are very pleased with her. She'll start her course in October. I am glad for her.'

Katharine realised that she genuinely meant what she had just said. Her mother's life would change once again, and so of necessity would hers, but she didn't feel frightened or threatened. She had become closer to her mother during the last weeks, as if the threat of losing something made you realise its worth. Her own life was changing. Soon she would have to make a serious decision as to which career she intended to pursue. She had always thought of medicine. She supposed she had wanted to live up to what her father might have wished. Now she was not sure.

She brushed her hair back from her face. A habit she was trying to break. The short curls round her face bounced back. She let them be.

'I'm thinking of leaving this year,' said Louise.

'What?' said Katharine and Jane together.

'You never mentioned it,' said Jane.

'I have a cousin who is opening a hair and beauty salon and she said she would give me a job. I'm going to work there during the summer holidays, and if I like it, I'll take a college course in October.'

'Why didn't you say anything before?' asked Katharine.

'I didn't say anything because I didn't want you to lecture me about my wasted potential, Kath.'

Katharine put her arms round her friend's shoulders.

'I am not going to lecture you. I think people should do what they are happy doing. I shall come to you for all my cosmetic advice. But only,' she added, 'if your products are made without cruelty. Anyway, look at the success of the Body Shop. You'll probably end up being a millionairess.'

'Don't be silly,' said Louise. But she seemed pleased.

The girls turned back towards the school.

'Do you think your mum will pass?' Jane asked Katharine.

'I honestly don't know if she's done enough work for it,' said Katharine. 'But at least she will have tried.'

'How was she this morning?'

'Dreadful,' said Katharine. 'I had to make the

breakfast and then she wouldn't eat it, and she would have missed the bus if Malcolm and I hadn't made the driver wait.'

'"Malcolm and I",' mimicked Jane. 'Now that's a significant statement.'

Katharine's face coloured up.

'He's a friend,' she said.

'I will be monitoring your behaviour closely at the disco, my dear. Number of dances, length of time together, distance apart during slow numbers etc, etc. All those tell-tale signs.'

Katharine thought ahead to the disco in a few weeks' time. Brian Patterson was definitely interested in her. If anyone had asked her six weeks ago whom she preferred. . . Now she didn't know. What a predicament to be in. She smiled happily.

They entered the school. Mrs Douglas had just finished talking to Mr Hogg and was going in to the hall.

'Aha!' said Louise.

'Never mind the "Aha",' said Katharine. 'My mum is going to concentrate on her career first and men second.'

'Come on, you lot,' Mr Hogg was checking his watch. 'Your mother is already in the hall, Katharine. You lot should be doing last-minute swotting, instead of swanning round the playground eyeing up the talent. Before you go in, is there anything you want to ask me?'

'Yes,' said Jane. 'Can I go home, sir?'

Mr Hogg ignored that.

'I'll be in my room later if anyone wants to come and see me. Good luck.'

The girls entered the assembly hall. There was the

low murmur of subdued voices. Katharine could see her mother sitting far away on the right-hand side of the room.

'I'm taking this seat,' said Jane, 'near the door, for a quick escape.'

'OK,' said Louise. She sat in front, and took out a calculator, a rubber, a ruler, two pencils, three pens, a paper hankie, a stick of chewing gum and a packet of sweets.

Katharine hesitated for a second.

'I'll meet up with you later,' she said. '*Bonne chance* and all that.' She crossed the room to where her mother was and sat at the table next to hers.

Her mother leaned over.

'I'll be all right, dear,' she whispered, 'you go and sit beside your friend.'

'I am,' said Katharine.